CW01633208

A ... STEPS MORE

CORRECTION, FREUD, JUNG'S, DARWIN'S

AND ALL ASTUTE

MINDS BLESS!

[illegible]

WED, 19 MARCH 2025

OF COURSE, WITH ABSOLUTELY

NO CHARGE

TO YOURSELVES!

LEE

WED, 19 MARCH

2025!

(OF COURSE)

WITH ABSOLUTELY

NO CHARGE TO

YOURSELVES!)

LEE

WED 19, MARCH

2025! LEE

A FEW STEPS MORE

LEE GERAINT INGMAN

This is a work of fiction. Names, characters, places, and incidents either are the product of the author's imagination or are used fictitiously. Any resemblance to actual persons, living or dead, events, or locales is entirely coincidental.

Copyright © 2023 by Lee Geraint Ingman

All rights reserved. No part of this book may be reproduced or used in any manner without written permission of the copyright owner except for the use of quotations in a book review.

First paperback edition 2022

ISBNs:
Paperback: 978-1-80541-417-9
ebook: 978-1-80541-418-6

For my mother.

1

Leaving the lonely loch behind, Michael, sober for the first time in a long time, considered his options as waves lapped along the shoreline. Usually, while in a retrospective mood, he would head for the local pub, but The Black Friar held no interest. After embarrassing himself in there just a few days ago, for once in his life, he felt a niggling sense of embarrassment. Suddenly, he had started to care about his own appearance and also what other people thought of him. This marked a big change in thinking for him. Spurred by his earlier conversations with Kate, he had started to care about, not only himself, but also considered the feelings and perceptions of others. And the bad habits which had brought him to this point. His mental recollections had begun to change and he started to think about his later years when his father had left the household.

Striding along the shores of the loch, a bout of daydreaming put him on autopilot as he began reminiscing about a certain day when a milestone birthday found him sitting on a swing on a damp and dreary autumn morning…

2

❖

Michael swung his legs back on forth, making the swing's chain links groan with the effort. Around him lay an assortment of discarded rubbish: cigarette butts, pop bottles and a plethora of other unwanted, disposed-of waste. It was five in the morning and the sun had just begun to appear over the horizon. As it rose, Michael did nothing but yawn, attempting, on some level, to groan himself awake while a light drizzle beat down on him from above. Nothing much stirred. Just him, the drizzle, a light breeze and his own jaded, disinterested interest in the world.

Birds had begun to sing and tweet from their places in the trees. However, this dawn chorus did nothing to lift his spirits; all he felt now was a low-key kind of boredom, a slight, but niggling, feeling of exhaustion and a reluctance to return home.

A walk of about a quarter of a mile now stood ahead of him. A few streets away, his bed awaited him and yet, although it was calling loudly to him, slipping between the sheets and falling asleep was far from his mind. Instead, Michael simply lit up another cigarette as he casually rocked himself back and forth on the swing.

In this sleepy little village, not much of anything happened. The streets were silent and deserted, the wind whipped the drizzle up into a disturbing ballet and yet, Michael felt a reluctance to stir. On the morning of his twenty-first birthday, he remained cold, miserable, bored and depressed and yet, as he got to his feet, they ended up taking him through the deserted streets of this sleepy little town and onwards towards home.

3

Back at the loch, Michael continued to stride along towards his temporary home. However, although it was late, he didn't feel in the least bit tired and also, without the booze, he doubted he'd sleep at all anyway. He'd been through withdrawal a few times in his past, but this time he felt a deep psychological need not to drink. Maybe his short but heavy conversations with Kate had altered his view of the world.

However, when he passed by the local pub, he felt a deep urge to cross the threshold and order up a pint and a few whisky chasers. Something stopped him though, so he strolled on through the darkness which was interrupted only by the glare of the streetlights casting an orange hue along the narrow roadway. This darkness seemed to seep right into his soul, draining him of emotion.

Having passed the pub, the cravings got a little deeper, showing off their resilience even though that tempting vision lay well behind him. For an inordinate length of time, he almost backtracked, thinking nothing of breaking his newly acquired oath. A day or so without the drink seemed to have hit him hard, but instead of changing direction, he continued on his solitary trip home. His determination was strong, a lot stronger than it had been in his past, and he had soon reached the entrance to the small B&B.

In his room, Michael stared out of the window and lit up a cigarette. Chain smoking again, he inhaled smoke after smoke until the pack was completely empty. Booze was one thing, but his failed attempts at giving up the fags had led to nothing. Medical doctors had recently postulated that tobacco addiction could be worse than heroin addiction and, having experienced both himself, he could well believe it.

With the pack completely empty, he had little choice but to ignore the need for more and climb into bed and sleep. Would he sleep tonight without the booze? He didn't know, but without that little helping hand, he doubted it. Regardless, he climbed into bed and, rather surprisingly, felt himself drifting off.

4

After that morning's episode, Michael had slept quite deeply, but eventually found himself lost and lonely within the confines of the house. Time passed along swiftly and the thoroughly welcome sight of the night, which now pressed heavily against the windows, was soothing. However, he quickly discovered that the familiar wave of depression he had experienced very early on that particular morning persisted, darkening his mood as he made the short trip to his local.

After an hour or so, he found himself sipping at his third drink of the night, drinking from a glass which was loaded with vodka and, of course, an obligatory smattering of orange juice. The pub was almost deserted, but still remained open, it seemed, for him alone.

Getting plastered was high on his list of priorities that night where, during these muted celebrations, Michael tipped his drink to his lips, drained the glass, placed it with some meaning back onto the bar and ordered up another dose of brain rot. The barman looked almost disapproving; disapproving that Michael hadn't offered him one in turn, he guessed, and yet he was soon preparing another drink for him to drown his sorrows in.

Suddenly, the door to the bar swung open, allowing yet another jaded, but thirsty, customer into this arena of utter gloom and despondency.

The clock behind the bar ticked its way to ten o'clock and Michael sighed a sigh of disinterest. Now standing next to him, this fresh face took off his jacket, shook off the rain, and ordered up a pint along with a whisky chaser. For a while, Michael allowed the newcomer to take in his environment. Although completely familiar to him, this new customer found himself staring rather pointedly at the bar clock; a short sixty minutes left to intoxicate his mind remained and yet both the pint and the chaser would probably last him until at least half past ten.

For a while, Michael ignored this fresh face. Ahead of him, Tim the barman poured Jim the postie a pint of Brains, sorted out a double shot of Glenfiddich and placed them onto the bar top. He sighed, and then rubbed his hands together expectantly. The local postie raised the pint to his lips, filled his mouth with the brew and swallowed deeply. Michael had become bored though, so instead of re-ordering, he drained his glass and, rather reluctantly, began the slow, monotonous walk home.

The narrow alleys were dark and this darkness was interrupted only by the sickly orange glow of the streetlights, his own shadow projecting onto the ground ahead of him and the weak glare of the moon. Within a second or two, however, he'd exited the alleyways and soon found himself walking along one of the town's main roadways, striding ever closer towards home.

For a while, his footsteps echoed all around him while his breath fogged up in front of his face. Home was now a few short steps away and, rather reluctantly, his feet continued to take him inexorably there despite his reticence.

Chimneys exuded smog and smoke from their enormous stacks; both from the street itself, but also from the adjacent industrial estate. A bottle of rum, he remembered, lay at his bedside table and navy rum just happened to be one of his favourites. A litre of Coca-Cola would have helped wash the liquid down by now, Michael glumly guessed, but it hadn't yet been touched.

At the front door, Michael dug out his keys, unlocked the heavy oak barrier and slipped past his slumbering mother to ascend the stairs to his bedroom. Once there, he uncapped the rum and, not bothering to mix it with the cola, raised the bottle to his lips and swallowed deeply. For a while, the liquid scorched his throat as it made its way down to his stomach. Michael sighed, took a long look out of the window and decided on yet another dose of fresh air.

The rear garden was both silent and deserted and, as he slipped once again past his slumbering mother, walking through the mist which blanketed the lawn, he headed towards the narrow, twisting river at the rear of the property. Trout, midges, owls and mice shared the space with him and, for a time, Michael simply gasped in the clear, unpolluted air which surrounded him. His father's lockup stood in a dark, shadowy corner of the yard, untouched now for a good couple of years and yet, although the subject of several fishing fantasies, the old and rotting structure now held little interest to him.

Over towards the meadow, nothing stirred and yet, Michael found himself imagining Mother Nature's influence on the pasture. The rum slipped down his gullet as he, once again, swallowed deeply, letting it tingle its way down towards his stomach. It had been a good few years since his father had left the property and Michael was grateful of the reprieve. Not having him around was a serious bonus to both he and his mother and yet, on some level, he supposed he still missed the bastard.

For a while, Michael simply sipped at the rum. Sounds from the stream reached his ears as he bathed himself in the relative silence. Out in the distance, traffic from the meandering roadway cut through this silence, but ignoring this, Michael simply sat on a low bench facing the stream while the battered rope swing creaked in the breeze. Above it, the old oak's leaves and boughs continued to whisper in the wind.

The rum, combined with the vodka and oranges he'd been drinking earlier, had now reached his head and, after a few stumbling steps, Michael left the yard and headed through the half-empty house and up to his bedroom.

From the bedroom window, Michael could see the dark outline of the neighbouring school; its structure bathed in the moonlight. The image of which he found both distressing and uncomfortable. It had stood in place on a small hillock which surrounded the town for a good few years now and, from this angle, Michael could see how the towering blocks of masonry cast dark shadows across the length of the roadway.

In the distance, cars passed by his window while he stood silent, choking on his own emotions as toxic fumes gathered at the roadside; remnants left behind by the exhausts of the passing vehicles crisscrossing the highway.

Strangely aware of this, Michael sighed a sigh of regret. Regret that the school was still standing, that was.

Down in the alleyways, smog and mist had formed, blanketing the still and quiet streets below him while, all the while, Michael held back the tears. Although his landmark birthday had now passed, Michael was still very intoxicated and so, not caring, he raised the bottle of rum, once more, to his lips and drank. His bed was now calling him, but he felt a reluctance to slip between the sheets because, being buzzed both by the liquor and a plethora of memories, something deep down inside him was calling him into action. He resisted this though. Instead, he simply lay on his bed, closed his eyes and slept.

5

Waking up, Michael turned his back to the window and wished for more sleep. The craving was still there, but as before, he mentally fought the urge to drink. Self-induced as it was, Michael couldn't help pitying himself on some level. Years of physical and mental addiction had caused these cravings, but they just couldn't be stemmed in any other way but through drinking. Trying not to dwell on this though, he got out of bed, showered and dressed himself slowly. Peeking out of the window, he shied away from the harshness of the sun, then opened up the window while grasping hold of a fresh pack of cigarettes.

While he smoked, he flipped the switch on the kettle and waited patiently for the water to boil. Once it had, he shuffled over to the bedroom table and poured himself a strong coffee. He was thirsty, but coffee wouldn't quench this particular thirst. As he sipped at the coffee, he became well aware of his physical condition. Was he shaking?

A thin line of sweat had appeared on his forehead. Jesus! Was this withdrawal? He supposed it was. But, ignoring this, he continued to smoke, but copious amounts of caffeine and nicotine just weren't doing anything to deflect his need for alcohol. Delirium tremens, he supposed. The pub would be shut for a good couple of hours yet, but even when the doors opened, he promised himself he wouldn't indulge and just go cold turkey. Decades of over-indulgences… no, *addiction,* he corrected himself, had gotten him here. Alcohol was a dangerous drug capable of alleviating worry and stress, but your own mind and body could soon become reliant on it. What he was feeling now wasn't just a bad lingering hangover, but the extreme shock of withdrawal.

The call to breakfast soon came, but Michael just couldn't handle eating; depression had kicked in again. This time it wasn't the liquor, but the actual absence of it. He ignored the breakfast offer, laced up his trainers and finished off his smoke. Rain beat down harshly and the wind accompanied it, blowing the downpour right into his face as he exited the B&B. Sitting on a bench facing the loch, he shook and did his best to overcome the cravings. As the pub opened, he saw a few regulars bustling in and wished he was one of them, but determination got the better of him and he soon decided on a short walk to help him focus on anything but drinking. The demon booze had been a familiar but habitual companion for the greater part of his life and its absence was now making him frustrated as well as mentally and physically sick. He had money in his back pocket, so that wasn't the problem, but his determination seemed to be stronger than the intense cravings.

He was soon walking back to the shores of the loch where a few fishermen were chancing their luck despite the dismal state of the weather. He paid them no mind as, not only was he in an anti-social mood, but he didn't want anyone else to clock his current state, shaking as he was like a junky craving their next fix. Which, he supposed, was what he actually was.

Even that small craving to see Kate again had now vanished, due to embarrassment, he soon concluded. So, instead of engaging, he quickly disengaged from the reality of this particular moment, sat himself upon a small hillock and let his mind drift.

6

The morning after his twenty-first birthday, thanks to the booze, Michael awoke with a serious hangover whilst harsh sunlight woke him from a very deep sleep. Downstairs, his mother seemed to be hurriedly making breakfast before her long and arduous day shift at the local bakery. Feeling a need to remain where he was though, Michael pulled the bedsheets up over his head and attempted once more to fall asleep. It wasn't happening. After a few winks, he pulled the bedsheets aside, stood up and began to dress himself.

At the breakfast table, his mum served up toast and cereal before leaving him alone in the kitchen. Bored, Michael decided on a short walk through the partially empty streets. It was now nine in the morning and his hazy head, made so by a lack of sleep and his hangover, was militating against his planned stroll. Despite this, he soon found himself reaching for his coat, tugging it on and stepping out into the rain.

Dark clouds were threatening a severe downpour but Michael ignored this threat as he picked himself through the streets of his hometown. His breathing was laboured, helped along by the cigarette he was smoking to help him wake up from the zombie-like state he was now in. The local shop was only a street and a half away and he reached it in a few minutes. As he paid in cash at the counter for another dose of nicotine and tar, Michael wondered what in the hell he'd do with the rest of his day.

The pub was an obvious choice. However, the prospect of strolling through its doors depressed the living hell out of him. Anyway, he'd still have to wait another two hours before they officially opened.

After disposing of his current smoke, Michael took the wrapping off his recently acquired pack of cigarettes and lit up once more, hacking and coughing again while he inhaled deeply. Passers-by looked at him curiously. His face was familiar and yet, seemingly out of place; he wasn't part of the morning rush endured by many who worked the day shift and also looked like death warmed up after his previous night of excess. Alcohol had once again made his head muddy and the prospect of sleeping off his hangover now seemed extremely attractive to him.

The town now seemed dreary, depressing and full to the brim with monotony, so Michael slipped past the curious gazes surrounding him and made his way homeward.

Instead of heading straight for his bed, he walked his way to the backyard, sat on the swing positioned below the boughs of the ancient oak tree and swung himself back and forth in an attempt to alleviate his boredom. Soon, he was surrounded by memories; memories of his childhood which was often spent harassing the trout in the local stream. For a time, he smiled widely, seemingly amused by past actions. The heavy branch of the old oak creaked in the breeze as Michael sighed. That had been a good decade or so ago and yet childish fantasies and mental actions soon filled his head.

The bubbling stream stood just a few short steps away from his father's rotting tool shed where a wide assortment of fishing gear resided. Sighing again, Michael fished out another fag and lit up, kicking out at the ground below him with his feet. He felt like burning that old, rotting shed down. To just stand there and stare as the whole thing went up in smoke. Yet, he remained exactly where he was, happy to just swing back and forth whilst he, in great detail, imagined the smell of burning wood as it crackled and popped, destroying a tireless amount of expensive fishing equipment which his now absent father had painstakingly acquired and accumulated throughout the years.

He had handled a few of the rods since his dad's departure, but the gear had lain neglected for the majority of the time. Fishing had been something his dad had encouraged and yet, the hobby now depressed him. Michael sat there musing on this whilst he both inhaled and exhaled the cigarette smoke into and out of his battered lungs.

Deciding to sleep, he left his perch at the base of the old oak and ventured inside. Heading towards his bed, his head was soon upon his pillow.

The rain pummelled against his window as he dozed. Frequently, his dreams were nightmarish and this morning, things were as per usual. He supposed that, partially at least, alcohol was to blame for this; his previous night's excesses had eventually caught up with him, he supposed.

The key to the school lay, as ever, tucked inside his bedroom drawer. For a few nights now, he had imagined making some sort of use of it. When drunk, he had almost done so, but for several years now, he'd allowed it to gather dust. Instead of utilising both it and the plethora of possibilities its use would provide, Michael had kept it at arm's length. Now though, he dreamt a dream which saw him making some use of it and he found himself pacing through the old school's silent corridors, looking for some sort of antidote to the emotional pain the place had instilled within him. There, as it did out in the real world, rain pummelled against the windows as he strolled through the main corridor and into the teaching blocks. White outlines of the teachers' notes peppered the chalk boards and the chairs lay at right angles to each other, silent and awaiting the strain of backsides on their seats while the shades were drawn against the worst of the downpour. All the while, Michael stood there, still as ever, shaking in both fear and anger.

The key had been useless to him for so many years. Ever since that dreaded trip to his headmaster's office and his short-lived attempt at rebellion where he remembered shattering the principle's cane over his knee. Temptation had called him into action and now it seemed, in this particular dream anyway, this temptation had gotten the better of him. He felt like tipping the tables, both physically and metaphorically, shattering the windows and causing as much chaos and damage as humanly possible. Suddenly, however, his dreamscape altered as he found himself bent double over one of the desks with his principal dealing out stroke after stroke from the birch cane which he always kept handy in a dark, dingy corner of his office.

That was the hardest part: crouched there helplessly while the headmaster berated him with harsh language as his spittle flew from the corners of his mouth, landing wetly on the floor as Michael cried out in repressed and unexpressed pain because crying out would just attract even more strokes of punishment. He never knew what he had done wrong in these dreams, but the punishment was always the same.

Out in the real world, back then, keeping up with his lessons had been the main difficulty he'd faced. Information kind of seeped out of his head, leaving him to stare quizzically down at exam papers or to stare out into space during the course of any average school day. No one knew the cause as well as him, but his daydreaming served as a release from the harshness of everyday life and, whilst unharmed out in the real world, his sleeping self relived these past traumas while raindrops slammed harshly onto his bedroom window.

Sleep eventually released him though and he found himself breathing heavily onto his pillow, gasping the air in and out of his lungs as he fought through the foggy remnants of his dream.

7

Back at the loch, Michael did nothing but sit and smoke. The wind blew harshly and the anglers seemed to be low on luck, but these were mere distractions and he knew it well. He was avoiding thinking and was cold on both a mental and physical level, but there he remained until the harshness of the weather caused him to stand up and continue his walk back along the shore; not for once exchanging a word with those who he encountered.

As well as fishermen, there were a few walkers, usually with dogs pounding the ground ahead of them. He nodded to them as they passed him by, but didn't pursue any kind of conversation, simply slipping past them, not for once expanding, or even attempting to expand, on these brief exchanges. He found himself in an anti-social frame of mind and, aside from the chill in the air, he realised he was now very hungry, so retracing his footsteps, he headed through the high street and arrived back at his lodgings.

After a few smokes and another few doses of caffeine, he decided on a trip to the local cafe. He could have headed to the pub for his lunch, but the temptation to drink whilst there would probably cause him to relapse, so having ordered, he sat by the window in the cafe whilst he drank a scalding hot cup of tea and waited for his food to arrive.

He vaguely thought about finding Kate again as his mood had now changed and, while he sat there, he realised that company, as well as a dose of empathy, was what he now craved. Low on both though, the only option which lay open to him was to allow his mind to drift and he sat there looking both sad and lonely for quite a while, filling the time up with nothing other than reflection.

8

❖

Following his foggy dream state, Michael found himself wandering the empty rooms of his childhood home. Lighting up another cigarette, he smoked almost incessantly before entering his father's study. Finding an ashtray, he puffed smoke up towards the ceiling, settled back in the room's solid leather swivel chair and closed his eyes. The battering of the rain still hadn't ceased, but Michael now found it to be extremely calming.

Although generally a place of woe, he'd experienced quite a few pleasurable moments within the confines of this room and, although contradictory, these memories caused him to think back to happier times. Times when his dad had educated him on not just life, but through the mainly solitary pursuit of reading. Back then, Michael had enjoyed these long talks; his focus shifting from one life lesson and onto the next. Although reading became a source of enjoyment, Michael's attention had been finely attuned to every snippet of knowledge his dad had chosen to hand out to him. It had done him little good out in the real world though because he'd been, and he supposed he always would be, a daydreamer, but sharing these intimate moments with his father had been a release from the harsh pressures of everyday life. On some deep level, Michael resented him, but spending time with his father had been a kind of therapeutic, unconstructive waste of time.

Still smoking, Michael was left with no other choice but to recall the harsh punishments his dad had subjected him to; most of which had been perpetrated within the confines of this very room. Scars peppered his back and, even to this day, Michael could still implicitly remember the anguish of those particular "punishments".

No one outside the family unit had known and yet, Michael was still averse, when sober, to inform anyone of these unpleasant aspects of his past. Maybe in the future he'd feel compelled to share these thoughts with others, but right now, reality had released its grip on him and he sauntered out of the study and into the backyard where he was immediately drenched with rain. Storm clouds had gathered above him and the town continued to be pelted with rain, blanketing the hills which straddled the town with moisture. He surreptitiously wiped away the tears which had begun to form at the corners of his eyes, blurring the external view while, all the while, muddying his own internal monologue which had habitually captured his attention for nearly every second of his every waking hour, throughout both day and night.

The swing at the bottom of the garden swung harshly in the breeze as Michael went back inside and stared back at the kitchen clock. One o'clock. Too early to be expecting his mother, but not too late to eat. As he prepared his lunch, Michael stared out of the kitchen window at the gathering storm and purposely thought of very little, allowing the moment to capture his full, undivided attention. Nothing was worth thinking about right then and he consciously avoided slipping into that deep and familiar feeling of melancholy whenever he was left alone. Instead, he allowed the gentle ticking of the wall clock to serve as a steady, calming metronome whilst he prepared his lunch: frying eggs while the toaster toasted a few slices of bread. The fridge held a plethora of sweet and savoury snacks, but simple egg on toast would suffice.

After buttering his toast, Michael sat on one of the stools within the kitchen-diner and proceeded to stuff his face whilst he casually glanced up at the wall clock. Half one.

He stood in the doorway of the bathroom, trying not to think of that traumatising yet insightful episode. It had been about twelve years since, but the whole thing seemed to him like it had just happened yesterday. He imagined the blood, the sickly sweet sight of his scarred father and the steady dripping of the bathroom tap. He should really get it fixed, but changing or altering *anything* inside or outside of the house was simply beyond his remit.

That old realisation about victims and victimisers sent his head spinning and, suddenly, venturing upstairs now felt like not just a bad idea, but also a very unhealthy one too. He would usually spend hours wandering his way through the house, lost in memory and looking for a reason behind the heartache, yet none could be found. He should have learnt this by now, but something deep inside him kept pressing him into wandering the house and its grounds looking for something which, in the main, remained intangible.

Feeling both lost and alone, Michael left the confines of the upstairs landing and descended the steps of the house's main staircase. Half the time, Michael had no idea what he was *really* looking for. Answers? Reasons? He had no clue as to whether either would be enough to lift him out of his melancholy, but he kept reaching out for both in a futile attempt at eradicating his own internal demons. Demons which had prevented him from shifting on in his life. Personally, if he were given the choice, he would rather suffer without the guilt, but the guilt kept pulling him backwards, always accompanied by an abundance of unanswered questions. Maybe he could have done something to alleviate his, and his mother's, suffering throughout the years, but he doubted it.

Time heals all wounds he'd been told, but each day, he felt like he was moving through a quagmire of guilt and regret. The extent of his suffering often caused him to wallow in this quagmire and, consequently, he often felt as if he could do little constructively with his emotions. Maybe that was what was holding him back. This guilt and regret often led to self-pity and self-pity, by its very nature, was extremely unproductive. Yet, he felt like returning to these obtrusive thoughts and the suffocating emotions they generated, time and time again.

Shaking his head, Michael felt like locking up and leaving the property, but instead, he simply lit himself another cigarette and, once again, headed for the kitchen. The remnants of the storm now pattered against the kitchen's window and the sky soon cleared. After a few minutes, birdsong began to pierce its way through the heavy, cloying silence. The hands on the kitchen clock now showed it was fast approaching two o'clock. Still too early for his mother to return from her day job. So, averting his gaze, Michael sighed a sigh of boredom.

He was currently between shifts. Fortunately, his landmark birthday had been split between his four on and four off shifts, but throughout the previous day or so, his boredom had caused him to look forward to returning to work. Machine minding seemed to suit him both mentally and physically. The work was light and undemanding and, aside from when the machines needed a tune-up or repair, he needn't have to speak to anyone. The mechanic was talkative though and so Michael always attempted to fix the problem himself manually rather than ringing the bell required to call him into action. Instead, he would while his twelve-hour shifts away by simply sitting down on a cheap plastic chair, staring ahead into space, filling his gaze with nothing but the lifeless, dead glow of each of the machines' display panels. Nothing intruded there. Not even during his breaks where he would hurriedly eat and spend the remainder of his break just brushing around and deconstructing the cardboard boxes in which the waste plastic would gather; a sad but pragmatic existence, he'd often thought.

Getting home was the hardest part though because he knew eight hours of sleep would await him. Eight hours where his memories and recollections would invade his mind and dampen his spirits. He was definitely what the classical poets had labelled as a tortured soul, and that's what he in fact actually felt like.

Losing this thought, Michael looked around himself at the still and silent kitchen. His stomach was full and was currently in the process of digesting his egg on toast and so that was a little distraction, but even without this, he felt a wave of melancholy hit him square between the eyes.

"Snap out of it, Mikey," he admonished himself.

What he needed was some sort of distraction, so after wrenching the kitchen door open, he stepped out into the yard, briefly registering the dying wind and the absence of the rain.

Surreptitiously, he headed towards the old, crumbling tool shed and unlocked its rotting wooden door with a little effort. The lock was stiff with time. Spiderwebs snagged in his hair as Michael drank in the sensations of damp, rot and the passage of time. Quite frequently, as like in that particular autumn morning, he'd imagined kicking down its door, hearing the splitting of the wood as rusting metal hinges gave way. Yet, right now, he was at a loss. Having been given the keys to the kingdom, precipitated by his father's departure, Michael now considered nothing but the slow passage of time itself… and a short venture into arson.

Irreplaceable fishing gear was staring back at him; remnants of one of his father's obsessive hobbies. Torching the lot of them was now uppermost on his mind, but he simply locked up the shed whilst the babbling of the stream snaking its way through the rear of the property reached his ears. Memories soon filled this gap in thought as they enveloped him within an overload of emotion. Dying driftwood lay haphazardly along the shores of the river, forming a dark, depressing tableau as he shifted his gaze away from its fast-flowing depths. These memories took him all the way back to the numerous fishing trips his dad had taken him on, strolling along the banks of the river and testing their luck upon its shores. Mostly, all they had caught had been little tiddlers, but on occasion, they had caught several large rainbow trout and Michael, full of youthful glee, had reeled each and every specimen in with great exuberance.

Hearing the rush of the river, helped along by the earlier downpour, Michael sighed a sigh of deep regret and loss. He could have easily pushed his father head-first into the river and make himself look completely blameless and innocent. The beatings would have stopped immediately and would also have provided him and his mother with that much-needed reprieve they had fervently wished for. Guilt, once again, filled his mind, but had he taken full advantage of the situation, would he have then felt even more conflicted? Confused, Michael turned his back on the river and tuned out the sound of its fury.

Back inside, he shuffled over to the stool he'd been sitting on throughout his meal. Sitting down, he again sighed a sigh of boredom. Instead of filling the void constructively, he glanced up at the wall clock once more, half two, and considered returning to bed. What he needed then was some sort of break in consciousness, but he felt averse to sleeping because, likely as not, nightmares would ensue.

At twenty to three, he locked up the house and strolled through the streets towards the familiar sight of his local. Ordering at the bar, Michael folded his arms as music blared out of the jukebox. Someone had selected a familiar album: Elton John's *Goodbye Yellow Brick Road* and he listened to "Bennie and the Jets" as he nursed his beer. The place was almost deserted since the lunchtime rush had ended and home time was still a good few hours away, so Michael stirred up a conversation with the barman. There wasn't much to discuss, however, so once the normal pleasantries had been exhausted, he simply ordered up another pint and listened pointedly to the lyrics of the title song.

"You can't plant me in your penthouse. I'm going back to my plough…"

It was now three o'clock. just another hour or so until his mother would return. To kill the time, Michael drank and drank until the stool he was sitting on felt wobbly and slightly unstable. He didn't want his mother to see him drunk, so switching from beer to coke, he allowed the rest of the album to play out before sauntering over to the ancient jukebox.

Knowing the track listings off by heart, he punched in D1. Soon "Fireball" by Deep Purple was screaming out from the speakers and Michael beat his feet in time to the music. A couple of pensioners looked over at him disapprovingly, but Michael didn't care and they were soon engrossed once more in their boringly familiar game of dominos. Sinking another cola, he was soon ordering up another one while he watched as the wall clock ticked away the last few seconds before four o'clock.

He'd leave soon and, a couple of cokes later, he was heading out of the door with a painful and slightly slurred "goodbye" emanating from his lips.

Coming home to be greeted by his mother always seemed to lift his spirits and he was soon engaged in a monologue of pre-emptive conversation. Unlike at his local just now, he would talk to the point of distraction with his mother, often feeling slightly guilty as she recounted her day while he sat back surrounded by a haze of disinterest. It wasn't the fact he wasn't interested per se, but he much preferred telling her all about *his* day and all it had entailed. Today though, there wouldn't be much to discuss apart from a long bout of boredom, an uneventful trip to the local and a good few hours spent in a state of denial, guilt and regret.

He'd think of something to say though, so at around about half past four, his mother returned from her day shift.

He greeted her at the back door, seeing the lack of enthusiasm in her eyes. Her shift had been as gruelling as ever, but she had been looking forward to returning home to her son who always welcomed her openly. Staring into her eyes, Michael was taken back to those times when they had looked just as dead as his father's. Beating after beating had caused her to latch onto her fate at the expense of most of everything else in her life, including, Michael thought rather morosely, himself. He couldn't hold that against her though. After all, something had to have gotten her through those long-gone, extremely trying times.

At the door, they embraced with some feeling and soon got to talking about each of their days and she was soon relating to him her gruelling day whilst he waited, with some patience, to speak. Soon though, he was talking, recounting in great detail his day with a lot of feeling.

Unfortunately, that look in her eyes reminded him of past events and, as he jabbered on, he couldn't help but think again about his father's short temper and general impatience. They had both borne the brunt of his anger for many years, decades even, but whilst his mother had found her resilience in religion, Michael had found it in blatant denial, breaks from reality and, later on in his life, in drink, drugs and the hope of a reprieve from his father's special, but far from rare, form of madness. Beneath the veneer, talking was also a good release from the pressures of everyday life, but it did little to heal bruises of the physical kind and the emotional scars which came along with them. Nothing could alter the past though, aside from the few futile attempts he often found himself loathe to recall or perhaps even to forget.

Just now though, maybe that was beyond his reach, but maybe, sometime in the future, he could bring himself to forgive his dad. Seeing his mother in a state of pain and anguish was hard to bear however. Nothing could alter the emotions he had felt soon after a beating. Neither he nor her could have reasoned with him no matter how much they both needed a breakthrough. His dad was rotten to the core and far from redemption. However, although his father had started to fall into the habit of writing to him, with some meaning, it seemed, to express his remorse, Michael had left the majority of his rants unread. Maybe he did feel guilty, but Michael certainly didn't possess the capacity to forgive him just now. That fall… push, he corrected himself, down the stairs had more than angered him; it had left him feeling incensed. Physically, his mother had broken a few bones, but mentally at least, she had become an equally broken woman.

Fear had held them back, but now they didn't dare discuss their treatment at his hands and, as he continued to recall his day, Michael felt that same low-key brand of anger he was extremely familiar with.

With it being autumn, darkness was soon pressing against the windows as Michael, now finished with talking, allowed his mum to recount her own boring day to him, diverting the feelings of woe which could have sparked the violent memories of both of their pasts. During the evening, however, Michael found himself simply enjoying his mother's company and little else. He was due on nights the following day, so after his mother had retired to her room, he simply watched the nighttime run of shows and tried not to think about drinking. He'd turn in soon, but for the time being, he smoked and tried to relax a little before bedtime.

The TV soon bored him though, so turning it off at the mains, he ascended the stairs, entered his room and crashed out on his bed. Soon, dreams enveloped his mind as he walked along the main corridor of the now silent and empty schoolhouse. Wind battered the building as Michael wished himself to be far away from here. Maybe, somehow, he had unfinished business there because his subconscious always seemed to take him back to this same point in his life. All around him there was silence; only the wind broke through. As he began the slow walk along the main corridor, Michael surreptitiously wiped at his streaming eyes; he was crying, but had no idea what had caused the tears. Beyond unhappy memories, that was.

It was always the same dream. Soon, he knew he would enter the same classroom and begin to experience the same guilt and regret which had followed him around throughout his formative years. These emotions did little aside from torture him. So, slowly but surely, his feet took him inexorably towards the entrance to the room as the wind howled through the eaves of the place. Still crying, Michael crossed the threshold, wiping, once again, at his eyes.

Instinctively, he knew what was coming, but those same dark emotions soared through his mind as he found himself doubled over his school desk while his principal admonished him with every stroke of the birch. Words of anger and chastisement pierced the air as Michael gasped out loud; each stroke registering with him on both a physical and emotional level.

Now craving complete consciousness, Michael attempted to pull away from this particular dream, but his efforts were futile. Nothing could take him out of this dreamscape, so he continued to endure the brunt of the headmaster's anger, feeling the pain as stroke after stroke was inflicted upon him. Soon, the ordeal was over with, but not the nightmare as the wind continued to howl and raindrops battered against the non-existent windows.

9

❖

Back at the cafe, Michael had soon finished his meal, had drank his tea and paid his bill, tipping the waitress a little as he exited the place. The sight of The Black Friar once more made him want to drink, but as before, he shook off this thought and simply headed for home. Maybe later he would bump into Kate, or she might decide to visit him.

In the meantime, he was left to endure his own company. So, after taking off his coat, he slumped himself down in the room's chair and lit up another cigarette. Staring out of the window, he thought of little as his breakfast was slowly digested within his stomach. He now felt a little more relaxed after eating. With that physical need now satisfied, he was left with only his coffee and his cigarettes to keep his senses sharp. Attracting sleep by lying down upon his bed was a no-no due to the fact he wished to avoid a sleep state where dreams were blatantly encouraged to manifest. He'd had a hard time with sleep, not just lately, but also, and probably thanks to the alcohol, in his past where they had been utterly disturbing and emotionally painful in their content. However, even now in a sober state, the memory of them continued to shock and distress his waking self.

Coming to the conclusion it was probably the withdrawal which was now torturing him, he allowed this thought to flit through his mind while he smoked incessantly between mugs of extremely strong coffee, just allowing the peaceful haze of the afternoon lull to distract him from other similarly invasive thoughts whilst he smoked and drank.

10

Waking in a sweat, Michael rubbed at his eyes as he stared across at his alarm clock: 3:36. Feeling slightly nauseous and a little off-kilter, he rushed to the bathroom and stared back at himself in the mirror above the sink. He looked worse than he had the previous night, but why he tortured himself in this way with the same dream, he had no idea. He didn't think he was any kind of a masochist, so why the same troubled sleep cycle? Something within him had to be telling him something, but what that was, he hadn't much of a clue.

His old principal had been jailed years ago, so revenge wasn't really within his grasp even if he had considered it. Although, he supposed, during those beatings, strangling the bastard was something he would often think about… slowly, that was. Being the man he was, however, thanks to the loving influence of his mother, maybe he had completely forgiven him for what he had done as his mum's preaching had given him the capacity for this. But, based on his own disturbing dreams, he most certainly hadn't forgotten.

Splashing a little water onto his face woke him a little from the haze, but the dream was still uppermost in his mind. Shaking off those particular thoughts was an impossibility, so maybe he should just attempt to completely and consciously forget. At the moment though, thoughts of his unfortunate nightmare drifted through his mind as he proceeded to dry his face with the bathroom towel. The remnants of his bottle of birthday rum sat on the bedside table and he was soon raising it to his lips. A different kind of haze was what he now craved, so Michael allowed the liquid to pass along the length of his gullet after swallowing deeply, gasping in the stale air as he waited for the brew to pass along his digestive system and reach the dark recesses of his own deeply troubled mind.

He drank and drank until, fairly drunk now, he collapsed once more onto his bed and wiped at his mouth, savouring the heavy, tingling sensation which was now stimulating both his stomach and gullet. He hoped he wouldn't dream and, not sure if he even had, he awoke just before his mother set off for work the following morning.

He was hungover, but his night shift wouldn't start for another nine hours or so. His body had the time to recover. For a while, he stared up at his bedroom ceiling as the front door shut quite audibly; the sound tearing through the silence as he purposely got himself out of bed, dressed silently and ventured down the staircase and into the entrance hall, study and the spacious kitchen. Strong black coffee followed as he thought about what he would do with his day.

Possibilities entered his mind and he systematically discounted each and every one of them, coming to the conclusion that, without sleep, he'd be bored. Not caring though, he trotted over to the sink and, now caffeinated enough, washed up his mug and placed it onto the draining board. Afterwards, Michael lit himself a cigarette with the window half-opened and wished he was somewhere, or someone, else.

Impotence had caused this feeling; he knew this better than anyone else did. Yet, he continued to smoke, recalling, in a great deal of detail, the ordeal of the previous night. Alcohol was a useful ally, but it didn't quite take away the pain and fear which he had, on some level, learnt to live with for the better part of a decade. No one else seemed to know or care about his melodramatic past, however, apart from his mother, but discussing his unhappy memories with her made her feel uncomfortable. He was sure of this because he could read her emotions as easily as any open book. It wasn't that she resented what he'd been through, as he surely did, but it was the fact she herself felt partly to blame for it and this included what his principal had subjected him to. When it came to that, she was utterly blameless, but Michael was sure as sure could be that she blamed herself for his father's actions. His dad was a grade one, thoroughbred bastard, but that hadn't been her doing. Rather, it had probably been the selfish actions of his equally morally inept grandfather which had precipitated his father's behaviour. Grabbing hold of the pair of them and shaking some kind of sense into them had been a frequent fantasy he'd indulged in throughout his younger years. His grandfather, now dead to the world and about as emotionally intelligent as he had ever been, had probably been the source of all the resentment and ill-feeling which he now harboured towards his equally morally inept father.

Something about this kind of knowledge was deeply disturbing, but his insights were often of this ilk, leaving him wondering how disturbed he actually was. Sleepless nights got him pondering these questions and yet, no tonic could mediate his own internal demons. Not even booze. He'd probably grow out of his resentment given time, but right now, he'd have to ride this rollercoaster of strong emotion until that particular day dawned.

At the moment, having finished with his cigarette, he ventured outside and sat on the old rope swing to ponder for a while; a habit which he had carried with him ever since the heady days of his own blighted youth. It was true his father had manipulated his emotions until they themselves had often felt totally alien to him, but he questioned this fact even then while trying to avoid the heavy philosophy which his morning had, hitherto, been composed of. Swinging in a dizzying arch below the boughs of the old oak, he allowed his mind to drift onto better times.

His mother had soothed him after each and every one of his father's "episodes". Even in his younger years, coming home to his mother's loving greeting had helped to heal a few of his wounds. Without this, he was sure he would have turned out exactly as his father had. Scars had been passed down for at least two generations, but with each passing day, although the hurt had somehow deepened, he felt like his mother's loving influence had saved him from a life of constant hurt which, although mainly emotional in nature, somehow filtered through into his dreams and especially into his reflections. Even now this hurt him badly.

Swinging back and forth, he thought for a while about the hugs and kisses she had bestowed upon him which then made him smile widely. The wind whipped him in a dizzying arch below the boughs and he smiled even wider as he recalled the happier memories his mother had helped to forge. At that moment, although she was only a mile or so away from him, this void seemed thoroughly incalculable. He wished to be near her, to see her love and compassion as she stared back at him with her doe-like eyes which he had also inherited from her. His shift would start at seven, but hers would end at four. So, in the meantime, Michael would have to find something to occupy himself with as, asides from depressing rumination, he had very little else to focus upon.

Maybe he'd find comfort in the words which his father, out of guilt, he supposed, had written to him. But he supposed that simply burning the letters might just lift his spirits, so after a misspent hour on the rope swing, Michael left the yard and headed back inside to retrieve the letters. Hiding them from his mother had been a difficult task emotionally, but also physically as his mother knew every nook and cranny both inside, and outside, of the house. They were currently hidden in his bedroom drawer; left there after each and every post day.

His mother usually left at around half eight, so Michael was the only one to retrieve each mail delivery when it arrived, almost always, promptly at ten o'clock each morning.

Getting himself a bottle of kerosene from the kitchen drawer, he proceeded to the mini barbecue grill which resided in the outside shed and tipped half of its contents onto the paper notes, then lit up a match and watched as they all went up in smoke. Grinning now, he felt a little better as his little paternally inflicted secret disappeared into the wind. Feeling better, Michael proceeded to blow onto the stacked papers, igniting them further as he smiled even wider.

Job done, he retraced his footsteps back inside the house and slumped himself down on the sofa, taking in a deep breath as he relaxed himself a little more. The house was silent, but this silence was rudely interrupted as he put on a fresh CD from out of the living room cabinet. Heavy bass shook the room as a dose of dance music screamed out from the stereo. It was one of his favourites and, aside from the jarring but melodic sound as it cut through the air, he relaxed a little more, taking in the quiet lull of the morning.

It was now close to eleven; his night shift wouldn't commence for another good few hours, but he decided to while away his day just listening to dance music and snacking from the fridge. Chewing on a thumbnail, he decided to mentally prepare himself for his upcoming shift by focusing on the sound of the music which would soon be replaced by the whirr of the machines and the rhythmic sound of plastic moulding being reformed into useful, and useable, items produced for the mass consumer market keeping the world afloat.

Soon it was time for his mother's return and he wrenched himself off the sofa and made for the back door. While she entered the house, Michael dimmed the music, which she had grown to dislike, and once more embraced her in the kitchen. It had gotten dark, but Michael could still see the exasperation in her eyes as she entered.

Her day had been as harsh as ever and, as she sat on one of the kitchen stools, Michael listened half-heartedly as she recounted her day. Given time though, the clock had soon ticked its way to six o'clock and he left her with a regret which was palpable.

Arriving at work, he shuffled through the break room and into the main production area towards his workspace in a shadowy corner. While he got himself settled, he surrounded himself with the sounds of the machines. Machines which he loosely regarded as lifeless friends of his; their gentle, hypnotic sounds soothing to him.

Clearing up, he brushed the debris off of their displays and swept up the waste that had gathered around them. Twelve hours of graft now stood ahead of him, so a little lost inside his own world, he got on with the job, keeping everything clean and tidy as he put in his earplugs and focused on little else apart from the simple task at hand. He was a good worker and was always diligent and yet, the twelve hours would sometimes drag. Seven o'clock was the magic number and for a few of his shifts, especially the first one, Michael would find himself clock-watching. That couldn't be helped though, especially when he would consider his options in what he could do to amuse himself for those dozen or so hours. Thinking could be a dangerous pursuit though, so wrapped up in his work, he did his best not to.

At 7 a.m. his work was done. Michael left his work area about as tidy as it had been left and headed for the bus stop. A short ride home took him to bed where, instead of waiting for his mum to rise, he fell asleep and dozed until around lunchtime. Head full of the previous day and with the sounds of the machines still whirring around in his skull, he ventured downstairs and got himself a makeshift breakfast in the kitchen. Tucking in, he stared out of the window at a gathering storm and wished to be far away. He started thinking again about his absentee father as he finished the last few morsels of his meal. Washing it down with strong black coffee, he felt fully justified in burning those troublesome letters the previous day, but instead of relief, a niggling feeling of guilt remained.

Should he feel guilty about some disingenuous ranting? Or should he have read each and every word rather than turning the lot into ash? What was his dad *really* after? He was so clueless as to the man's ultimate motive and true purpose in regards to him that he felt lost, lonely, afraid and about as helpless as he had felt as a child.

Thinking about all of this, and how his dad had now made him feel, he felt angry but also impotent. Did he seek forgiveness or was he just trying to worm his way back into his affections and, if so, then why? Still angry, Michael lit himself a cigarette and tried his best to cancel out this deep-rooted feeling of rage as raindrops slammed up against the windows. A storm front engulfed the small hamlet as the outside temperature dropped. From his perch inside the dry kitchen, Michael felt a kind of relief as his thoughts were diverted to the weather, but still a niggling sense of anger kept him rooted to the spot.

Seven full years had passed since his dad's departure. He'd left them with the home and its contents, but also with unpleasant memories and a heavy reminder of his presence. A presence felt deep inside the house and home which he now shared with his scarred, frightened and rather jumpy mother. Their nerves had been frayed and they were constantly reminded of their patriarch's brutality, but on a wet and windy mid-autumn day, both hate and anger enveloped him and caused him to scream out loud. Something he hadn't done in years. Although relief was felt by both, nothing could combat the fear and righteous anger they both felt quite regularly towards him. Even simple, daily pursuits had sometimes had to be abandoned in favour of the fear. Nothing, it seemed, could alter this.

High on this negative emotion, Michael silenced his scream and wandered into the bathroom to shave and shower. Running the blade across his face, he attempted to divert his thoughts. He felt like crying, but kept completely silent as his dad would then, once more, have succeeded in getting to him. Instead, he showered in tepid water and attempted to master his emotions. Uselessly, he dried himself with a towel, dressed and headed back down to the kitchen. The wind was howling now as heavy raindrops pummelled the window whilst the old oak tree swayed in the breeze.

The next few days passed in a blur and, aside from a few nightmares and another long spell of boredom, Michael felt good about being alive. Another letter had arrived through the post though, doubtlessly from his father, but Michael had neither opened nor dared to read it. It currently resided within his bedroom drawer, hidden from his mother who would undoubtedly get upset at its very presence within the home.

His night shifts were done with for now and, after placing the letter unopened inside his drawer, he once more came across the key to the school, waiting patiently and staring back at him from its hiding place. He'd use it tonight if things went as planned. A jaunt back to his childhood was definitely on the cards, as if going back there would slay some dragons. So, Michael busied himself in preparation for that trip, thinking about everything and nothing while his mother occupied herself indoors. Her weekend had just begun and, having worked hard all week, she was left with nothing more to do than keep the house in order while he proceeded to sleep his entire morning away within his bed. Greeting her at lunchtime, they embraced once more as Michael did his best to conceal the unasked for, and unwanted, letter from his father. He succeeded. So, Michael ate his lunch and thought of little.

Seeing and interacting with his mother without hindrance was a bonus, so after a productive afternoon spent in her company, nighttime came around and he was soon heading for bed where, instead of sleeping, he waited for the sounds of slumber to emanate from his mother's room. After an hour or so, having heard the unmistakable sound of her snoring, Michael slipped on his trainers and retrieved the key.

The town was dead; only the soft echoes of his footsteps filled the void. No passing traffic and nowhere to hide, he thought morosely. Light rain beat down on him from above and his clothes were soon damp, but he managed to escape the extremes of the weather by entering the old schoolhouse. Afterwards, memories and unsavoury recollections filled the space between his ears as he glumly walked from room to room with his head still stuck in the past. Dancing shadows and the sound of his own heartbeat filled the space while a torrent of thoughts bounced in and out of his skull. He knew this was just another futile attempt at coming to terms with what happened, but he couldn't quite help himself and he continued to stride through the empty rooms. A few times, he felt rather nauseous, given his thought processes, but nothing could alter this as memory after memory danced its way through his head. He wanted to annihilate each and every last one of them, but instead, he felt compelled just to roam, searching for answers to questions which continued to elude him.

What the hell was he doing or trying to do? Here he was stuck in a gloomy old school looking for some sort of philosophical answer to his life and life choices; a twenty-one-year-old man who found it hard to accept his past and past actions. His dad had left which should have served as a bonus to him now, but nothing seemed to have changed, he realised, as he strolled from room to room. His principal hadn't helped the situation, but he should have forgiven and forgotten him by now. Yet, neither of these things seemed to have happened and he continued to cry as he dwelled on his past. He felt like burning the old school down, but was averse to doing so because spending years in jail for this crime wouldn't help his mindset in any way. At three in the morning, he left the old schoolhouse, making sure to lock it up behind him as he headed for bed.

Having reached it, he lay down and closed his eyes. His previous actions had left him drained and he was soon sound asleep, but back at the old schoolhouse, bent over a desk once again enduring yet another beating.

11

With a full stomach now diverting his thoughts, Michael craved company and he decided to try to find Kate again. As he finished off a cigarette, he laced his trainers and headed out. The sky had cleared now, but the pavement was still damp from the earlier downpour. The town was also deserted and, as he walked, his footsteps echoed hollowly which, had he not been alone, he most definitely would not have noticed. He still didn't know precisely where she lived, so instead of making a house call, he decided to scout the place where they had met up together the previous day.

Things were just as silent at the old bench facing the loch, so he simply sat down and waited. In the distance, he could soon hear a dog barking loudly and quickly realised it was Barney, Kate's dog, who was the culprit and he was soon stroking the mutt who had only just properly met him the day before. Dogs were so trusting, he thought as Kate sat next to him on the low bench. He was still shaking a little, but he still attempted to hide this fact from her. Kate soon noticed though and, direct as always, she commented on his unenviable condition.

"You've decided to go sober?" she asked.

"Pretty much."

"It'll get easier eventually."

"Right now, it doesn't seem that way."

"Every change is difficult," she replied.

"It certainly is."

"You'll be fine."

Michael frowned. "I hope so."

His earlier epiphany about needing people soon came to mind as he stared back at Kate. Would their budding relationship end up in sex? Did that matter? His lifelong interactions with the opposite gender, apart from his mother, had centred on sex, paid or unpaid, but with Kate, although she was attractive, their budding relationship didn't seem to depend on this kind of physicality. Rather surprisingly, he found himself even more interested in her thoughts and opinions, even those that focused upon him.

Right now, although that curious thought had flashed through his mind, his libido, dampened by the withdrawal, took a back seat next to the physical and mental symptoms which were now about ten times worse than his worst hangovers. He latched onto Kate and what she had to say while trying desperately to stave off that deep urge to drink. So far, he had resisted twice and, despite the withdrawal, he, on some level, felt almost proud of himself. At that moment, the decades-long understanding and sympathy which his mother had provided him with was what he really craved. Maybe, as he had thought the previous day, Kate could plug this gap. There still existed, and had for some time now, a vacant place somewhere within his heart.

High on this thought, he felt a deep compulsion to embrace her, but not only would this be wholly inappropriate and creepy, it would also be very premature. That is, if their relationship progressed. So, feeling a little detached, he once more took in her beauty and smiled a grim smile. Nothing much else needed to be said, so despite his interest in Kate, he was soon backtracking again.

12

Harsh sunlight once again roused Michael from a very light sleep as he threw his bedclothes aside and got himself dressed. Three days of freedom now awaited him as his next lot of night shifts were that far away. What he'd do with that time though, he had no idea. Maybe he'd hit the pub and poison his mind a little, but the thought of this soon depressed him, so he left his room with his head buzzing with this thought. Downstairs, his mother was making a hurried breakfast; her own shifts left behind for another day or so.

They embraced. Michael felt a little helpless and immature, yet her comforting touch soon made him feel a little stronger. Outside, things were bright but a little breezy and the old oak swayed in the breeze; the sound of which stirred up a few memories as he choked back a tear and wiped away at his eyes. Nothing much else to focus on.

He felt a deep compulsion to keep hold of his mum and never let go, but he knew this was just a childish wish. Feeling for a place of safety which just couldn't be reached anymore, intangible, hopelessly lost to the ravages of time. Just as his mind was stuck in the past, so too were his dreams, hopes and reflections. Suddenly, the thought of just letting go was overwhelming, to just leave everything behind in a whirl of pity, self-doubt and, of course, that ever-present fear which continued to haunt him on a daily basis. He remembered his disturbed night with that same dream which returned to him time and time again and felt like screaming. With his mother present though, this wasn't an option. Instead, Michael sat down and ate the hurriedly prepared breakfast which his mother had made and attempted to empty his head of all of the negativity.

His trip to the old schoolhouse hadn't really helped. The nightmares had returned, leaving him feeling weak and helpless. Although these feelings were far from strange to him, he was soon reflecting on his dark past while he ate. This time focusing on a beating which had been far from his mind for several years now. It had included a trip to the study where his dad had been testing him on his latest home schooling task. This time it was the novel *For Whom the Bell Tolls* by Hemingway. *A Farewell to Arms* had been his favourite book by that particular author, so maybe he harboured a streak of sentimentality within him. *For Whom the Bell Tolls* had its moments, but Michael had much preferred the heavy melodrama of *A Farewell to Arms* as it reminded him of the often strained relationship he had with his mother. His dad was responsible for this though because often, when he sought out the comfort of his mother, his father would intervene and swiftly stop this kind of affection.

Things weren't going well because Michael had hardly grasped the plot, never mind the meaning behind the story. It all seemed to be hard drinking and philosophical rumination which frequently reminded him of his own dad's mindset. Alcohol would frequently undo all of the good work the quality time with his dad seemed to generate and so, his impatience whilst drunk was something he had learnt to fear. It was hard not to mimic this impatience, so Michael did his absolute best to be as patient and understanding as he possibly could be, not only displaying tolerance at home, but to his detriment, also within the schoolyard. He'd become an easy target for the unscrupulous elements of his school faculty by tolerating this abuse, but he just didn't want to be like his dad in any way. It was hard at times and he couldn't help but feel rage and also engage in bouts of imaginary revenge, thinking about dealing out some of the same to his classmates, father and sometimes also to his own teachers.

Getting back to his dad's home schooling, however, Michael attempted to remember what the book had actually been about whilst insight into his father's character once more streaked through his mind. It wasn't the fact he hated his dad though, he was forgiving in this sense, but it didn't take anything away from the fact he often couldn't quite remember what he needed to say to him whenever he was tested on his recall of literature. Hemingway could be a hard read and understanding every nuance of his writing and what he had probably implied was often a hardship. A beating soon ensued thanks to his poor recall, so Michael attempted to drift away, to leave the agony of his physical pain behind while staying doubled up over the desk like the victim he had become. Suddenly, he hated literature because it was entwined in learning; the kind of hard learning his dad often enforced through the beatings. Yet, on some level, he did gain a certain kind of pleasure in the solitary pursuit of learning which reading did provide a person with. Both being educated and literate was what pleased his father for some warped reason. This somewhat satisfied his need for some kind of paternal nurturing, but at that moment, he hated his dad with a passion. However, his deep desire for vengeance remained unfulfilled, yet it was still ever-present. Words at that moment failed him, so he continued to endure his beating as stroke after stroke of the birch rendered him mute.

Being immune to his own emotional state was what he really craved though because, without that, he was as vulnerable as ever to his dad's attacks. Not beatings, he corrected himself. That was what they really were. Despite his good intentions, his dad was probably paving a way to hell for himself.

Back in the present, this pain, grief and sorrow flooded his mind as he chewed his way through his hurriedly prepared breakfast; something which he just couldn't help but focus on. His father had humiliated him on a physical, mental and emotional level, yet he was still breathing and with every heartbeat, he told himself, he was getting stronger and stronger. "What doesn't kill you…" he'd been told. However, this grief, pain and despair was, and had been, killing him for years, he reminded himself glumly, sipping away at his coffee while trying not to let his state of mind be known to his long-suffering, though completely understanding, emotive and empathic mother. It was true to say that empathy connected the pair of them on a deep level, so passing over his problems through voicing the reflections he was experiencing was a no-no; she was probably as distressed as him anyway having gone through the same with his father.

Completely unassuming, Michael washed up and tried to focus on the lighter moments when his father had been absent, but the wind whipping against the branches of the old oak and the crazy ballet which the swing was now performing made him reflect on his younger years where the comfort of that particular rope swing would send him spinning in a dizzying arch beneath the ancient tree. He needed some sort of release, so after washing his plate and cup clean, Michael trotted outside and, saying a hurried goodbye to his mother, began to walk. The fresh air soon filled his lungs as he pumped his legs hard uphill, making the walk into more of an exercise as he was getting a little podgy around the middle due to his lack of exercise in general… and his boozing, of course. Sleep would also come a lot quicker if he shifted himself, so with this in mind, he made his way uphill towards the apex of the town: the top of the hill which surrounded it. Once there, he took in the view but a sickly sweet feeling enveloped him as he stared downwards, surrounding himself in memory as he, once more and rather pathetically, wished to be near his mother.

He remembered childhood jaunts to this hillock where he would spend his time wishing to be far away from the town, but that wish had more to do with one particular inhabitant, his father, rather than the rest of the population as a whole. The locals were, in the main, kind and considerate, yet these traits did nothing to redeem them in Michael's eyes because they were all blind to his suffering or knew about it and had chosen not to act. Michael hadn't known which one had been worse: not knowing or knowing and not caring. Ignorance seemed to be bliss, he thought as he took in the scene.

Without realising, he found himself sitting atop the hillock and lighting a cigarette almost instinctively. As he puffed away, smoke dissipated into the air as he surveyed the town below him rather critically. It was a sleepy Sunday with little passing traffic and not much to really focus upon. However, church bells began to chime below him, cutting through the deep lull of the afternoon. He took another long drag of his cigarette and remembered his own childhood mornings spent throughout sunny summer days inside that stuffy old chapel as he watched the town's dwindling congregation exit that particular house of worship.

He'd hated being there, but with his mum being a devout Christian and his dad a long-suffering acolyte, he'd had little choice. With his dad singing his way through yet another hangover and with his mother silently wishing for his demise, the vicar would then sermonise his way through the yawns and fidgeting of the younger children of his flock. Faith, especially Christian faith, had been responsible for many of the world's ills, but there they were, praising God and trying to worm their way into both his affections and, he supposed, heaven itself. Hypocrisy all over, he reminded himself, while watching the group depart; the vicar rounding them all up like sheep every Sunday morning… or like lambs to the slaughter. He knew he was bitter and had a streak of cynicism present within him, but the fact remained that no one knew what, if anything, lay beyond the veil, but childish hopes were what kept his boat afloat.

Finishing off his cigarette, Michael tossed it aside and took in another few lungfuls of the relatively unpolluted air, but his mood had shifted. He felt angry and upset about something intangible to him, although his previous thoughts had probably… likely, he corrected himself, contributed to this shift in mood.

On the short walk home, Michael passed by a few ramblers braving the cold. He'd wrapped up warm and they too sported scarfs and gloves along with their heavy boots and thick socks. They were so engrossed in the scenery they hardly even noticed him as he passed them by. He was grateful for this because he just didn't feel like conversing at all with anyone and only wanted to get back home; small talk with strangers wasn't part of his agenda today.

Having walked the half-mile or so back downhill, Michael, back home now, popped on the kettle and was soon sipping at another mug of strong coffee. The fact remained that he had no itinerary for the day, so while he drank, he thought about all of the things he could possibly do with his time. Clueless, he talked with his mother a while and then trotted out to the garden.

The breeze had almost turned into a gale now, so it collided harshly with the old oak and the wooden swing swaying below it. Suddenly, that old depression seeped back into his mind as he strolled along the edges of the old path while he took in the sight of his childhood home remembering little, feeling little and thinking about little; a brief but intense reprieve from the thoughts which usually held him in their grip. That old barren yard required a lot of upkeep, but he wasn't in the mood for that today; the weather, and his state of mind, also precluded this essential maintenance. All along the yard the grass was ankle deep and the old washing line, barely used now, swung violently in the breeze as he lit up yet another cigarette, coughing harshly as the smoke proceeded to hit his lungs. The depression was getting to him, however, so ignoring these thoughts, he re-entered the house and, still thinking about little, ascended the stairs and, ignoring his mother for a second or two, he crashed out on his bed.

Dreams soon filled the void as he left consciousness behind, allowing his emotions to take charge as he surrendered his thoughts. He found himself playing out in the yard after a beating. That day had been a violent one; his inability to correctly interpret *For Whom the*

Bell Tolls had had its consequences and Michael felt this in his back and backside as he went about his play-acting whilst trying hard not to dwell on this failure. It was only a book and yet, it seemed to hold special significance to his father who remained over-obsessive about literature. Sure, Michael enjoyed reading because it involved the use of imagination, but figuring out the ins and outs of a novel didn't always come along with the practice of reading itself. He liked to enjoy a book, regardless of its content, and yet his dad still insisted on analysing each and every yarn from the inside out.

It was a pity he didn't do the same with the contents of his own psyche, Michael thought glumly. Despite this, he often enjoyed his time alone as he could quite easily drift off into whatever fantasy came to mind during these short periods of time. Today, he was a pirate, avidly defending a territory filled with the crashing of the sea and plenty of stolen loot. Surrounding him was the dead and dying driftwood from the old oak and the choppy surface of the river which tended to double as a vast open ocean during his many jaunts into the fantastical.

Living like this often cut through the dullness of his day and, often, when he was done pretending, harsh reality intruded, but he didn't want to think that way for a while now. Instead, he bounded through the yard, imagining himself, cutlass at hand, fighting off a steady stream of opponents. On some level, he was just glad his mind hadn't taken him back to that dusty old schoolhouse, so unhindered now, he continued to relish the freedom which the backyard often afforded him.

Michael's play-acting had taken him, temporarily at least, away from his nagging, self-destructive thoughts for a time, but his mother was soon calling him back inside and Michael, still stuck somewhere inside this dream, followed the pitch of her voice to the back door. He was soon immersing himself in warm embraces which did little but bring back that old and familiar feeling of helplessness. Still, he relished the moment, but was soon falling away from his mother's clutches to land face first into the empty school's corridor where the familiar battering of the wind and rain came to his ears. He, as usual, expected the worst and he was soon receiving it as he awoke in a puddle of sweat.

Surprisingly, dusk had fallen and Michael was soon traversing the stairs to greet his mother in the downstairs hallway. She soon informed him that he had slept his way through five hours or so, yet it felt like just a few minutes since his head had hit the pillows. He'd probably lose a few hours of sleep that night because of this but he wouldn't, or didn't intend to, return to the old schoolhouse to fill in this time. His dad's unread letter still resided within his dresser drawer, so maybe he'd read and pick it apart during this time.

Deciding on a quick drink after his unfortunate dream, Michael unscrewed the top of a bottle of wine and filled both of their glasses, filling his to the very rim and downing it like pop. His head was soon spinning and he proceeded to crash out on the sofa while his mum took to the lounger. They were soon taking in the boredom of that evening's television schedule; the programmes dulling his mind just as the wine was doing.

It wasn't too bad an evening because just being in his mother's presence usually did the trick, but she was soon retiring in light of her day shift which would start the following morning. This gave Michael little to do but while away the rest of his night with the TV on. The nightly broadcast soon bored him though, so instead of remaining in front of the screen, he ascended the stairs, flopped down on his bed and retrieved the letter.

Preparing himself for a gush of sentimentality and supposed regret, Michael was surprised by the letter's contents. Apparently, his dad had started work at the stock exchange and had included a few notes in currency as if to prove this. Michael retrieved his wallet and quickly stuffed the notes inside it while he digested the contents of the rest of the letter. Having a bottle of wine to hand though, the printed words soon lost their clarity and became muddled. So, depositing the bottle on his bedside cabinet, he closed his eyes and drifted off.

13

Sitting on that damp bench next to Kate, Michael felt like their fleeting conversation was over with, but that didn't matter. Just sitting there next to her seemed to be enough. They continued to take in the silence. It was a similar feeling to those moments which he had shared with his mother as they had both smoked and enjoyed the quiet lull of the backyard of his former home; nothing needed to be said and they were both content to just sit there quietly as vocal expression wasn't really required.

He was still shaking slightly, but Kate offered no further comment and he liked her even more for this. Huddled together on that bench, Michael ignored his craving for a cigarette, but also felt a deep need to drink. He'd fight until this want had dissipated though. Succumbing to that intense craving now would not only make things even more complicated for him, but would also damage his own fragile ego and his trace amount of self-esteem, which had been severely battered by the drink throughout the years. Suddenly, he was doing his best to hang onto the small amount of self-respect he had gained following a day or so of sobriety. He and Kate needn't say anything about this aspect of his own self though and, as the waves continued to lap along the shores of the loch, a piercing silence continued to surround them both.

It had just struck two in the afternoon and, with his earlier meal digested, Michael felt the pangs of hunger once more. With the local cafe now closed for business until the following morning, there wasn't much choice left aside for a pub meal. With regret, and with a little trepidation from him, they both headed to The Black Friar for a late lunch. Resisting the need to drink, Michael selected a corner table and they were soon sitting down to eat. Remembering the oath he had made to himself, Michael sat sipping at a diet coke while Kate nursed an orange juice.

Looking around, Michael, now an ex-drinker, couldn't help but feel not only regret, but also a deep feeling of sympathy for those who he considered to be tied to the bar. He saw on the faces of some of them that painful mark of addiction. Social drinking wasn't their problem, but *habitual drinking* certainly was. He hated this thought because, on some level, he was placing himself upon a pedestal as an equal amount of sympathy was somehow entwined with his deep feeling of regret. Could he make it? He sipped at his cola while he secretly wished it was also topped up with a strong dose of rum.

For a time, he and Kate engaged in small talk but their food soon arrived. Kate had learnt from her previous meal at The Friar and so she hadn't ordered herself a vegetable curry again, but rather a meal equally bereft of meat… a vegetable lasagne. Michael had a steak with a smattering of chips, mushrooms and onions and they were soon silent once more, stuffing their faces as Michael, again, attempted to ignore his craving for a drink, trying his best not to get up and saunter over to the bar for a pint or two. Instead, he continued to sip at his coke while he ate heartily, filling up his stomach with something which wasn't laced with alcohol.

An hour or so later, both of them stuffed, they decided on a little stroll along the loch with Kate's faithful companion, Barney the sheepdog, accompanying them. Michael, with his craving for a drink gone rather temporarily, still shook, but his resolve seemed to have hardened and he kept pace with Kate and the mutt while they engaged in more small talk but this time Michael was soon pressing her on the premature death of her mother. Both of their mothers had died young, relatively speaking, but the pain and anguish of both of their deaths against the backdrop of their conversation kind of lessened this pain and anguish on a deeply spiritual level.

Talking was a kind of therapy. He'd learnt this years earlier, and so they continued to engage for the majority of their short trip along the shores of the loch; Michael catching snippets of their conversation and committing most of what she had to say to him to memory. It seemed now was the time for *her* to bear her soul to *him* and he found himself listening intently, almost on a par to how she had listened to his telling of his own melodramatic moments related to his past just a day or so ago.

Time soon caught up with them though and, rather regrettably, Michael parted company with Kate as he reached the doorway to his temporary home. He invited her in, but she blankly refused and he was soon flopping down on his bed, shaking, but not in the least bit tired. Usually, he'd head for the pub in moments like these, but tonight, he was at a loss as he sauntered over to the window and lit up another cigarette. Smoking, he hit the button on the base of the kettle and waited for the water to boil and, once done, poured himself a strong dose of caffeine, but the heavy hit this provided him with, along with a large dose of nicotine, just wasn't doing much for him. Trapped inside his own headspace, he sipped at his coffee and attempted to leave his present position behind.

14

Later on that night, after a refreshing sleep, Michael soon found he needed a drink, so deciding to hit the hard stuff again, he ventured downstairs, unscrewed the top off a whisky bottle, raised it to his lips and swallowed deeply. Soon, the tingling in his stomach had become a tingling in his head and, as he flopped down on the sofa in the living room, his thoughts were quickly diverted as he was overcome with a deep feeling of detachment, an urge to forget, but none of it seemed to matter now as he continued to drift off into relative apathy.

It was still a good few days until his next block of shifts at the factory, but he thought once again of his job, which seemed to suit him, and the hours which would be occupied with him predisposed to thoughts akin to that of any jaunt into the fantastical; just sitting there mulling things over until clocking-off time at seven in the morning when he'd take the local bus back to his home which he shared with his emotionally scarred mother. His only problem seemed to be sleep as it usually opened up the floodgates on certain memories; memories which he always tried his hardest to suppress.

Soon though, Michael had drunk as much as he could that night and, leaving the now empty bottle of booze on the coffee table, he found his thoughts were now dulled as he strolled through to the kitchen and, now standing at the back door, smoked heavily while his head became dizzy. He'd been drinking for the best part of five hours or so and this session had been a heavy one. Not caring though, he flipped the cigarette out from between his fingers and sauntered back off to bed. At six in the morning, he decided on a few extra hours of sleep.

15

❖

With nothing left to do but smoke and drink coffee, Michael whiled away the rest of his night alone in his temporary home. He thought about heading downstairs to watch the television, but his need for the company of others had waned, so instead of heading downstairs, he found himself enjoying his own company, which he now preferred compared to the complications always inherent in human interaction.

At around nine, he decided to turn in early and he was soon surrounded by dreams which were far from regressive. Instead of dreaming about his dubious past, he imagined a time where he hoped past events wouldn't take centre stage and where he could live on happily without a mindset which was always churning up hurtful memories. Maybe his budding relationship with Kate would become more than just a passing friendship. Maybe fate had brought them both together; he with his weary soul and her with her liberal insights on life and the living. That was what he *really* craved: someone to be there for him, to take the reins on his future rather like the way his mother had on his past. Sobriety had also seemed to take the nightmares away and, while he slept, nothing but positive emotions filled his dreamscape so by early morning on the next calendar day, Michael woke up completely refreshed and found himself thinking rather positively about his future.

That morning, after washing and dressing himself, he sauntered downstairs to the breakfast table and proceeded to fill his gut. Stomach full, he conversed with his temporary landlady for a while and, after locking up his room, left the small B&B and crossed over to that same old rugged-looking bench. Craving company, he wished once more for Kate. Social interaction of the kind Kate could provide was what he now found himself pining for. After a few smokes, his wish was granted, but instead of talking about both of their gloomy pasts, Michael was left with the urge just to relay his brewing positivity to her and they talked about the possibility of both forgiveness and the possibility of redemption. He was still shaking slightly, but the urge to drink had faded. For the time being anyway. They talked for a good few hours more while Michael also fought to ignore the urge to smoke; new research had recently highlighted the dangers of passive smoking. Breathing in the clear mountain air, Michael proceeded to enjoy these moments with Kate as they both stared ahead of themselves at the choppy surface of the loch.

Time moved along quickly, a change since time always seemed to drag whenever he was alone, and it was soon early afternoon. The weather quickly changed, so caught up in a burgeoning storm, he and Kate decided to head inwards. Inside the B&B, they both sat quietly in the television room and watched boring repeats on the screen until his landlady offered them both a brew. She sat down and, during a break in custom, disclosed the fact Michael was now the only resident. Instead of making him feel privileged, this admission made him feel lonely and slightly vulnerable. But vulnerable to what? He now had Kate and his funds were far from low, so why those particular feelings? Nothing came to mind and he was soon caught up in the moment, thinking about little as he interacted with the two other souls gathered around the box.

16

To put it mildly, Michael had fucked up! Leaving a half-read letter from his father, rather stupidly, on his dressing table, his mother had found it and read its entire contents. With a face like thunder, she had confronted him the next morning. After being pressed, he soon disclosed the fact there had been others. After relaying the contents of these to her, he quickly admitted, not only to a small dose of sympathy for his absent father, but also to that of a small pang of guilt which had left him feeling emotionally conflicted.

Having a mostly liberal mindset, she allowed her anger to dissipate as Michael began to relax a little as he rekindled, along with her, the vengeful thought processes they had both found themselves experiencing since his departure; those which had also probably kept the both of them sane. Afterwards, he found that, not only had his disclosure been a weight off his mind, but that little pang of guilt, when vocalised, had also dissipated.

After a good heart-to-heart, Michael felt wholly vindicated now that everything was out in the open. Did he still hate his dad? Curiously, that small hint of sympathy he had harboured towards him had stopped him from hating his father in a complete and unwavering way because how could you hate a person you pitied? So, after an hour-long discussion, they both nodded in agreement with a promise that he would hand any future correspondence immediately over to her. The letter itself, although only half-read, was then relegated to the barbecue pit; soon burnt to ashes as his mother cried over, but also prayed for, his father and her absent husband.

He felt like drinking, but staved off this craving by embracing his mother who was still in the long and arduous throes of forgiving. Beneath the veneer, Michael was sure she would take secret delight in any and all of his dad's personal woes. Christianity could quite easily manifest into hypocrisy if a faithful person was to stumble; morals seemed to be relative, but according to the "good book", they were all set in stone, unwavering and all-encompassing. Once her tears had dried, Michael's mum headed inside for a quick brew where they both attempted to forget their earlier discussion.

Michael felt a weight had lifted from off of his shoulders now his dirty little secret had been aired and shared. How would his mother react to the next letter though? On some level, Michael wished she wouldn't read it because he hated to see her crying no matter how conflictual the source of those tears actually was. Instead of drinking those thoughts away, he simply sipped at his scolding hot brew as they both bathed themselves in the relative silence.

Everything out in the open as things were now, Michael began to relax a little, saying very little about anything else in their lives.

17

❖

That night would end up being one of the worst of his life. Having left Kate earlier and with nothing left to do before today became tomorrow, he smoked at the window while his shakes were soon accompanied by a fast heart rate and cold sweats. Before long, not only did he sweat, shake and shiver, but he began to hallucinate. Perched by the window, these unpleasant aspects of an alcoholic comedown soon got him thinking about his past; he was well used to strife and hardship, but what his unconscious mind ended up concocting was at the extreme end of this scale.

His father, long dead now, materialised in front of him. Sitting down on the bed, he both chastised and berated him in a way which frightened but also angered him. The walls seemed to ebb and flow in time to his words while Michael covered his eyes and wished himself far away from his shoddy room within a cheap B&B situated in the heart of Scotland. He'd been carrying demons around with him for so long now, but his frequent nightmares weren't a patch on what he was now experiencing. The man was holding a sturdy and very familiar wooden cane and he beat it into the palm of his dominant hand precisely and unwaveringly in time with his words. Nothing could equal the torture of those moments except the actual experience itself.

Left as a child again, Michael, in some sort of regressive state, was reminded of his father's special kind of madness as he began to weep quite openly, turning his head away from this unwelcome apparition. On a very basic level, he wished for an end to his own conscious state, to just abandon his senses which were the ultimate source of his agitation and anguish. Despite this, he couldn't help fearing his dead father as he had feared him as a child. His equally dead mother was absent, but her loving influence upon him would have quickly negated this particular waking nightmare.

There was a lot of time left until the crack of dawn, so putting his head in his hands, Michael, his heart beating ferociously, sweat dripping from his forehead and shaking madly, stared back at his father as this threatening presence glared back at him with venom. His dead dad wasn't really there. He knew this implicitly. Yet, those same feelings of helplessness and hopelessness caused him to focus on the negative aspects of his life. He knew what would help him: a drink. His resolve hardened, knowing submission would only get him back in the rut he had created for himself within the past few decades. So, for a full ten hours, he endured everything which came his way throughout that long and lonely night, falling asleep for only a few precious hours before waking up with a lingering and unshakeable feeling of depression.

18

Afterwards, long after he had shared all of the correspondence which he had received from his father, the relationship between Michael and his mother seemed to strengthen. On any average day, they held nothing back from each other and he was glad to have shared his little secret with her. With everything out in the open, he began to relax in the few days left before his next block of shifts.

In the kitchen, they shared a long breakfast that Tuesday morning as the sun's rays shone mercilessly into the room at the rear of the property. Soon, his mother left for her day shift at the bakery, leaving him alone once more inside that creepy little house. Creepy because of the memories it seemed to trigger within Michael, and with little else to do, he smoked at the back door, allowing the smoke to dissipate into the clear morning air.

It was around half ten when the post arrived but Michael, not expecting anything of interest, suddenly wished it hadn't. Not so soon after his disclosure anyway. Another blue envelope arrived with his dad's neat handwriting scrawled across its front. For a while, Michael held it in his hands, debating whether he should open it there and then or allow his mother to do the honours. Curiosity got the better of him though and in a single moment, he tore open the envelope and began to read his father's neat, handwritten script.

What the hell did he want from him? Michael again wondered as he read its contents, filled with the usual bout of supposed regret and guilt. Could he really forgive him? His mother, on the surface, at least, had seemed to, but he was certain she held onto feelings of vengeance and hate because these would be a thoroughly natural reaction to her past experience.

Afterwards, Michael, shut up in a cage inside his mind, felt like burning every page, but handing it over to his mum would further cement their bond, so he placed the open letter on the kitchen counter in anticipation while the wall clock ticked away the hours left before her return. His dad seemed to regret the way he had treated them both and the nature of his departure seemed to hint at some sort of feeling of guilt. Exactly what kind though? Whilst he had left them both with the house, a smattering of savings, a series of bad memories and nothing much else, Michael's take on the past remained as it was: a clear-cut account of abuse with no abatement, internal struggles and a view of the world in general as something to fear. His conflicting perspective of his father remained unchanged, however, so while the rest of his day was filled with nothing but TV and his own personal collection of LPs to listen to, the clock inexorably ticked its way towards four thirty.

Arriving at the back door, Michael and his mother embraced once more and he soon showed her the letter and allowed her to read it. Conflicted again, Michael wished he had burnt the thing to ashes as he could plainly see the tears once more gathering in her eyes. It was up to her what she thought and Michael couldn't influence her any more than he could control his own emotions. She was upset, this much was clear, but he could do nothing to alter this. As the letter was relegated to the barbecue pit with a smattering of kerosene to help it along the way, it was then he realised the depth of his mother's feelings towards the bastard. Any attack on her personally, she could forgive, but any attack on her own son could never be excused.

19

Waking up physically and mentally drained, Michael just couldn't face breakfast, so donning his jacket, he stepped out into the rain on a gloomy and dismal winter's morning before finding himself craving a smoke. Lighting up, he wandered over to that same old weather-beaten bench with a conflict in his head and a sickness in his belly. Comedown was a bitch apparently. He hadn't felt this rough in a long, long time, but his resolve soon hardened when, like it or not, he was overcome with pride and a desire to please. Not only himself, but also Kate too who, quite surprisingly at the moment, he didn't crave the company of. He looked worse than he felt. He'd discovered this with a fleeting glance at himself in the shared bathroom's mirror. After half an hour's worth of smoking and repressing the urge to vomit along the shores of the loch, he got himself up and strolled along its banks, wishing all the while he was invisible.

The shakes were getting worse than ever before and he soon found his hands now couldn't even hold a cigarette. Although strongly craving a smoke, he, rather unwelcomely, attempted to endure, not just his extreme craving for alcohol, but also that of the fallout from his nicotine-starved bloodstream. Luckily, the loch was deserted as he just didn't wish to be seen in this state; being clocked as an alcoholic on a comedown was something he wished to avoid. However, Kate seeing him in this state would be far worse than a complete stranger doing so. Attempting to endure this unpleasantness by doing his best to ignore it, Michael continued on his aimless walk along the shores of the loch.

Last night had been hell. Seeing his father, unmarred by death and sitting right across from him, within touching distance even, had been a nightmare which hadn't been lessened by the knowledge he'd been an apparition without substance. A childish but totally natural reaction by him during this encounter had been that of fear and impotence.

Trying to forget this, Michael continued to stride ever forwards between the gorse and heather which the narrow walkway effectively cut a path through, but being starved of nicotine and alcohol, this act of forgetting was extremely difficult. Somehow, he managed it and he was soon walking along with an empty head. Now a good kilometre away from the town, Michael allowed the slight breeze to caress his face while all the while he found himself thinking about little of anything of any consequence. A very real outcome of an alcoholic comedown, he knew, could be death, but for a while at least, he felt more alive than he ever had been. So much so that, despite his mood, physical shaking and general shabbiness, he actually looked forward to returning home, taking a shower and then hopefully conversing with Kate a little later on in the day.

After an hour or so of wandering blindly along the shores of the loch, he re-entered the B&B as the only customer, took that shower and, after locking his room, wandered just as blindly over to that weather-beaten bench with a head which was slightly clearer and now expressed the need to talk itself into some sort of consolation. His state of being, following an hour or so of waiting, was injected with hope as Kate appeared in front of him.

She patted him on the shoulder and eventually asked, “How are you bearing up?”

He didn’t answer her for a while, just shook his head while he thought of a reply, but eventually said, “Didn’t you say things were going to get easier?”

Kate smiled for some reason, a reason which alluded him, before saying, “I did use the word ‘eventually’.”

For a while, Michael was silent, but he soon asked her a question which he needed, quite desperately, the answer to. "Why are you bothering with me, Kate?"

Without even a blink, she answered. "Because you're not beyond redemption… and I quite like you."

A question hung inside his head for a good few seconds before she added, "As a person, that is."

Michael shrugged. Sex was off the cards then. Surprisingly, this thought flashed through his mind without any accompanying feeling of disappointment because he'd just come to the conclusion that sex wasn't relevant to their relationship. In fact, this made their budding bond that much stronger. Sex, for so long now, had just meant the satisfaction of a physical need to him and had been far removed from the spiritual craving which had been left neglected by him throughout the last few decades of his life, lost within the daily consumption of a glut of alcohol and an accompanying dose of self-pity.

Stroking Barney who sat patiently by her side, Michael reminded himself of how Kate might just have saved his life. A life which could, quite possibly, have expired within an utterly legal drinking establishment. This sudden realisation kept those *other* thoughts at bay and, for a long while, he and Kate watched on silently as a cold breeze circulated along the edges of the silent loch.

20

A few days passed, but no more letters arrived and Michael was glad of this because, even though things were now out in the open, he still felt like a kid who had been caught with his fingers in the cookie jar. He needed his mum, so didn't want to court her disappointment even though he knew implicitly this would take some doing given the fact she was an extremely forgiving person. So much so that it was often to her own detriment and, even though he could quite easily have taken full advantage of this fact, he never had, not even as a child. Most kids were manipulative with their parents, usually by playing one off against the other to get what they wanted, but not him. His intellectual and emotional maturity were both strong elements of his psyche, but he had never made use of emotional blackmail and hardly ever made use of guilt trips. Yet, he was still naive in some ways. Trust was his main problem; trusting the good in people and, consciously or subconsciously, seeing next to nothing of the bad inherent in the heads of others.

His shift work would recommence soon and, in a way, he was glad to get out of the house and be of some use. Getting out was also important because he still harboured a trace amount of guilt gained through his lack of disclosure which, whenever he was in his mother's company, would reignite and make him feel uncomfortable. Thinking of this, he dearly hoped his dad's words were fully honest and truthful. Although Michael continued to do anything but excuse or rationalise his actions, he still wished his father would find some kind of happiness at some time or other throughout the remaining course of his life, although thinking in this way probably contradicted his true emotions. Michael was well aware of this dichotomy though, especially within the last few days whenever he had looked deeply into his mother's eyes. He'd also remained relatively sober for this amount of time, successfully resisting the pull of the local and the dark recesses of his dad's wine cellar. At around six o'clock on that mid-week evening, he trotted off to his job at the local industrial estate, carrying with him his box of sandwiches and the usual pack of twenty Marlboro cigarettes.

What was good about that particular week was the fact his mother had booked a few days off from her job and would be staying somewhere up the coast in the company of a few work friends. He'd been planning to do something for quite a while now. Something which he didn't dare do while she was present. So, on a damp and dismal winter's morning, just after he had gotten back from work, he found himself sitting and swaying on that old rope swing located in the backyard for a while. Then, in a rush, but still with premeditation, Michael retrieved a can of petrol from the outside shed and proceeded to dowse the entire contents of it all over his dad's lockup and fishing gear.

Standing back for a second or two, he allowed this particular moment to slowly pass, savouring and nurturing it before striking a match and throwing it dead ahead of himself. As it landed, flames began to lick their way skywards and Michael began to laugh. He had a fire extinguisher in his other hand, but left it quite a while before dousing the flames with the white foam. Then he took in the view while the ashes were still smouldering.

He felt extremely pleased with his actions because the lockup had become just one more reminder of his father's abuse. However, nothing but the white foam, soot and scorched wood now remained. He'd lie to his mother though, probably by stating he'd become careless whilst stubbing out a cigarette. However, he was sure she would secretly receive this story with cynicism as the both of them would somehow know he had done it on purpose. Michael was also sure that seeing that unpleasant reminder of her husband's placid, unassuming hobby had distressed her and might also have caused her a certain amount of pain, as it had him. Leaving the remnants of his little act of arson to smoulder in the frigid air, Michael crossed the yard and headed straight for bed.

21

❖

Michael and Kate sat at the edge of that particular loch for a good few hours, just talking. He wanted to ask her about certain elements of her own past, especially in relation to her father, which she hadn't, so far anyway, even mentioned. He wondered why this was so because her omission was concerning to him, but what could he do? Mention him? Prod at her until his curiosity was satisfied? Not at the moment, he thought, as they continued to talk about nothing. He had quite quickly and in some detail told her all about him, so why the reticence? However, Michael soon realised that, given the state he was now in, she would probably continue to focus on him. She was a good person, he surmised and not for the first time. It was all self-induced, but Kate didn't seem to mind this; her compassion suddenly felt utterly limitless to him.

After another hour or two, while they continued to chat about nothing of importance, Kate disappeared with her dog and Michael found himself sighing. Their little talk had passed half of the day away, but suddenly, Michael couldn't resist filling up his gaze with the sight of the local pub; its sturdy wooden doors remaining teasingly and temptingly open. He saw a few of its punters standing outside, between their pints, smoking their cigarettes and laughing over a story, joke or personal jibe. Thanks to the distance between him and them, he couldn't quite hear them clearly, but for a fleeting second, he wondered whether he might be the ultimate source of their amusement. Paranoia, probably as a result of his alcohol withdrawal, quickly got him thinking about what a shabby mess he must look to others.

Luckily, this particular train of thought was brief and, to a large degree, Michael was grateful for this. The temptation remained though and he suddenly felt like breaking his oath. However, the dry spell he himself had instigated quickly reminded him of the reasons behind his decision. How could you battle against a habit which, on some level, had kept you going throughout the course of a good few decades? With will, he reminded himself.

So, with the shakes now partially gone, Michael allowed himself one more smoke while he took in the sound of the loch, which was much more audible now the majority of the pub's customers had finished their smokes. Leaning back on the bench, he glanced down at his watch and discovered it had just gone six and also realised that not only was he hungry, but also that the local shop was about to close for the night. With some haste, he made his way over towards its entrance, went inside, and bought a few snacks which should serve to last him until the call to breakfast the following morning. He paid, donated his change to a cancer charity and headed home.

He stayed awake for quite some time, avoiding his bed and the need to sleep. Eventually, he rather reluctantly slipped between the sheets and surrendered himself to the nightmares which were now the usual norm for him.

22

His mother had enjoyed her little trip to the coast and she arrived back home with her mood having been lifted. Secretly though, once she saw what remained of the now non-existent lockup in the back garden, her elation went up a few notches. Michael saw her trying to suppress a grin… and she almost succeeded. Even without this visual cue, Michael knew instinctively that her reaction just about fell short of pride; pride he'd had the guts to incinerate this strong reminder of his dad's madness. They then spent most of that day simply eating and sipping at coffee in the kitchen where the view from out of the window provided nothing but a scene of soot and ash given the fact that was what remained of the lockup: the rods, reels, line, floats and various other fishing materials forming a decimated tableau of destruction. In short, this lifted both of their moods and Michael soon took on board that vague sense of pride emanating from his mother.

Michael also knew that, had it not provided a safe place for them both to live, burning the entire household down would go a long way to eradicating most of the ill feeling they continued to feel towards their, now absent, patriarch. On a purely personal level, doing the same to the school, which was still in operation, might just help to similarly eradicate the same ill feeling he still harboured towards the place. That was another story though and, although he often thought of actually doing so, he doubted he'd ever have the guts to.

With both of their spirits lifted, Michael went out into the backyard and lit himself one more cigarette while he watched with glee as the wind whipped through the burnt and mangled wreck of the shed and allowed himself a smile. His actions were fully justified, he thought whilst inhaling and exhaling the smoke which would undoubtedly further burn and scar his already battered lungs.

For now though, little else mattered apart from his elevated mood which had been brought about by his little act of arson. Expressing rather than suppressing your emotions, he'd learnt, was extremely healthy and, it seemed, very therapeutic.

23

Surprisingly, there were no more nightmares that night and Michael woke up feeling refreshed, but with no idea as to how he would spend the remaining sixteen hours of his day. Not caring, he ate his breakfast inside the downstairs dining room, showered, brushed his teeth and stepped out into the rain. Instead of waiting for Kate next to that old wooden bench, however, he walked over to his car which was parked up in a side street, got in and decided on a drive. He hadn't yet explored the rugged-looking countryside surrounding the town and, after a few minutes, he was heading through the hills and glens which cut a clear path between the ominous mountain peaks and the steep inclines which had formed at their bases.

For a while, Michael thought about leaving the little town and Kate, and his little jaunt into sobriety, behind, but soon reminded himself that, while he had left his childhood home for the unknown several months ago, that decision hadn't so far gotten rid of the recurring and conflictual slew of thoughts which had muddied his mind for all of his waking days and slumbering nights. How could you run from yourself? With much difficulty! He soon corrected this thought. It wasn't only difficult, but nigh on impossible!

Losing this thought, Michael drove on for another good few miles and, stopping his car in a passing point on a rugged corner, decided on a short walk. The pathways along the bottom of the ridges, however, were barely visible and sometimes completely indistinguishable from the heather and gorse, so he found himself struggling with every step. He didn't mind. He could do with the exercise, he thought as he walked his way through the harsh landscape.

After a while, he settled himself down by sitting on a hillock as he proceeded to watch the passing traffic, which was minimal, shutting off his mind for a second or two and allowing himself to enjoy the peace and quiet of the place. Eventually, he got up, returned to his car and found himself thinking of Kate and their budding and so far non-physical relationship.

Once again, he surprised himself by realising sex hardly mattered to him anymore, but the whys and wherefores of this feeling of detachment were totally elusive to him. Throughout his life, his, almost exclusive, interactions with the opposite sex had been nothing more than purely physical. Had other people in his past been willing to help? Had he also ignored and dismissed the help offered by so many others out of selfish and self-absorbed reasons for decades? He quickly dismissed these thoughts while he retraced his footsteps and drove himself back to town, trying his best not to think or feel anything which might muddy his mood.

Fifteen minutes later, he parked his car up in the same spot down a side alley, exited and walked the few steps home. The fresh air had done him good, but another fourteen hours still remained of his day, so avoiding the pub once more, he boiled himself a coffee in his room and slowly sipped at the near-scalding liquid as he smoked out of the window. Mere moments after he finished his smoke, however, the sight of Kate sitting on that same old wooden bench came to him, along with another bout of shaking and, for a time, he considered his options. Should he go out and greet her, or was he better off just ignoring her along with the heavy thought which her company would surely generate?

Regardless, he decided on another dose of her company and he was soon leaving his room, walking along the corridor and lighting up yet another cigarette as he walked over the cobbles towards her. He now felt like talking, but not about himself, he soon realised.

That new curiosity relating to her father had returned, so sitting down beside her, he purposely attempted to steer the conversation away from himself and his troubles while doing his best not to shake. In his alcohol-free system, the cravings returned, but they were less intense. Was he now a recovering alcoholic? Or was the chatter simply masking his need for a drink?

This craving, now relegated to the back of his mind, was pushed aside while he talked and, after an hour or so, he had built up the courage not only to just hint at the subject, but to ask her directly.

"What about your father?" he asked with a little trepidation.

"He's dead," she replied without missing a beat, adding, "Thank God."

With this, Michael realised they had at least one thing in common.

Staying silent, he gave her the chance to elaborate, but she didn't. She just sat there with, what he strongly suspected was, a heavy heart. Michael found his curiosity quickly waned. There was a story to be told here, but right now didn't seem to be the time. As they continued to sit and talk inconsequentially about nothing, the awkwardness drained out of the situation, leaving two lost souls to gather together around a small wooden bench which happened to be facing an equally small Scottish loch straddling a lonely Scottish town. Soon, Michael discovered life could, sometimes, at least, be a lot less complex than it frequently seemed.

24

❖

Still feeling slightly elated at his little act of arson, Michael spent his remaining day of freedom by cleaning up the mess left over in that corner of the yard. He was enjoying this immensely and was soon disposing of the burnt remnants of the rotting lockup along with the scorched and now useless fishing gear. Digging up a small trench, he filled it in with the soil which he had gotten from the bottom of the garden. Next, he sprinkled a few grass seeds onto it and, later on, allowed the rain to drench it. With the empty shell of the remains now cleared, he picked up a metal bin in which he had placed everything and made sure it was dumped beyond the sight of the house.

Even happier now, Michael wandered inside and was soon sipping at a coffee while he watched the gathering storm darken the skies outside. Safe and warm inside, he thought of his mother's muted reaction to his handiwork. He had sensed relief and a certain amount of pride towards him. He was very accomplished at clocking her mood and, ever since her return, his feelings had been affirmed and reaffirmed several times. He had also spent those days in a pretty sober state as drinking would have just spoilt the high he was now feeling. He spent his last few hours of freedom by preparing himself for the upcoming bank of night shifts in relative silence while he walked from room to room, for once thinking nothing of his father. Certain actions were highly cathartic, he'd found.

His mother soon arrived home from her day shift and they proceeded to enjoy this same silence because there was nothing left to say between them. After an hour or so, however, Michael headed out once more to arrive at work to waste yet another twelve hours of his life in the pursuit of being useful to the world. He was too intelligent for the work he had chosen, but had committed himself to the same boring job simply because it afforded him silence and, with it, the time to think. He was also a very simple man with no great ambitions because he'd found that most of his ambitions were satisfied within his own *internal* world where things were safer and a lot more predictable.

However, on that particular night, he had kept up with his machine and had done his very best to clear up the space in which he worked while he, simultaneously, allowed himself to revel in the simplicity of his life, thinking hardly anything at all about his future potential and finding himself totally focused on his current state of being. Luckily, the twelve hours soon passed him by and he returned home feeling a lot happier about his life than he had felt for a good few years now. Smiling widely, he let himself in and found his mother lying barely conscious on the kitchen floor.

25

❖

After his chat with Kate, Michael arrived home and soon discovered he, once again, was left with nothing else to do apart from smoke cigarettes and drink coffee. Looking back, he was glad he'd had the guts to quiz Kate about her relationship with her now dead father, but having gotten little else from her apart from that one small snippet of information, he was left feeling a little disappointed. Why was he so interested though? He supposed the real reason behind this was the fact that, through airing and sharing, talking openly about your life usually strengthened the emotional bonds between people. He'd learnt this well through the two-way relationship he'd had with his mother and, eventually, came to the conclusion he now wished for a similar relationship to blossom between himself and Kate. Should he expect more from her though? It was up to her, he supposed, but Michael preferred that she open up to him as and when she felt the inclination to do so. He decided not to force the issue upon her, but rather, let her decide in her own time whether she felt she trusted him well enough to tell him a little more. There was still a story to be told though; he knew this implicitly judging by her strong emotional reaction to that one slightly intrusive question.

For a while he did nothing but mull this over. However, what soon interrupted these thoughts was a shaking of his hands and a strong feeling of nausea. Rushing from his room, he quickly covered the space between himself and the upstairs toilet. Just about making it, he dropped to his knees and emptied the contents of his stomach into the bowl. His withdrawal seemed to be sporadic in nature; one minute he'd be fine and the next he'd be shaking, sweating and kneeling in front of a toilet puking his guts up. Kneeling there, he silently wished for it all to be over with, but supposed there was no way he could be spared the shakes, nausea and general gloom of his withdrawal. He was definitely paying the price for a decades-long spell of hedonistic abuse and maybe, ultimately, he deserved it all… and more.

It was now nine at night and darkness pressed up against the windows. He'd wasted about two hours through thinking, ruminating and puking, so after brushing his teeth thoroughly in an attempt to get rid of the sour taste of vomit, he lay on his bed and did nothing more than wish for sleep. For a long while though, he simply stared up at the ceiling, shaking, sweating and continuing to pray for some kind of alleviation… but it never came. Once again, he craved a drink, but quickly dismissed this craving through the realisation he'd come too far to go back now. He seemed to be at the point of no return, so quite stubbornly, he endured and suffered until sleep once more claimed him and was soon falling away from himself.

26

❖

In a state of panic, Michael rushed towards his mother. She was breathing heavily and, checking on her pulse, he found it was decidedly slow. Panicked by her condition, he rushed for the phone in the living room; not liking leaving her, but realising this was an absolute necessity. Stuttering down the phone line, he quickly reeled off their address and the nature of their emergency.

Returning to his mother, he knelt by her side and prayed. This was unusual for him as he knew his particular type of religion didn't include any supreme being testing the faith of the masses from some heavenly cloud in the sky, but he prayed now out of fear; a fear of losing the only tangible, deep-seated relationship he had ever known. While they waited for the ambulance, he stroked his mother's greying hair affectionately and spoke softly to her, telling her things would be fine even though there was no real assurance of this.

She was attempting to speak to him, but her efforts were weak. She made no sense at all which upset Michael further, so still stroking her hair, he allowed the fear to take over. It engulfed his mind with anxiety and trepidation while they both waited on the ambulance which had been promised to them. It took about ten minutes, but this relatively short span of time seemed to drag on forever while he held his free hand in his mother's, which was shaking. The fear which Michael felt, which was probably echoed by his mother, persisted even as she was wheeled into the back of the ambulance and, as he took a seat next to her towards the rear of the vehicle, he stared at the machine monitoring her heartbeats. The display unit built into it showed her pulse was, as he had suspected, too slow.

Luckily, throughout the short trip to the hospital, her heart rate started to increase, so that was something, he found himself thinking. Still at her side, he wondered what had caused this condition in such a generally fit and healthy woman. She was both a smoker and a drinker, but even this was in moderation, unlike Michael, so why the sudden shift?

A short time later, with his mother having been admitted onto a ward, Michael sat, both concerned and fearful, for a good couple of hours while blood samples were taken and while X-rays were performed. Her heartbeat slowly returned to normal, but Michael was still in a panicked state and he continued to hold her hand while they both sat there upright and rigid, continuing to hope and pray. Her breathing was a little lighter now and she continued to make quite an effort to communicate with him. However, her words were still random in nature, making no sense at all to either him nor the medical team attending to her.

The wait for the blood test results and scans took a good few hours, which felt like days to him. He sat in silence, not for once giving up on the hope which had been brought on by a strong feeling of concern. When the results arrived, the news was bad and, for a few moments, Michael had to clear his mind while it sank in. Cancer.

For a while, he actively refused to accept this diagnosis. Tears formed in the corners of his eyes as this realisation hit home: painkillers, prayer and the eventual realisation that death was probably certain would surely follow. After his mother had been discharged back to their home, Michael realised their roles had now reversed. Him, now a carer and a sounding board for her alongside the unwavering conclusion they were now immersed within a pitched battle between hope and the final eventuality of acceptance.

27

Engaged in a conversation which flipped in function between the trite and the serious, Michael and Kate sat on that same low bench and watched on passively while waves lapped around the edges of the loch. With that question asked by him the day before still unanswered, Kate, he strongly suspected, had expertly diverted any move towards the discussion of her dad by focusing, once more, on him and his woes. For a time, he found himself playing along. There wasn't any other choice, he thought between sentences, because the further cementing of their relationship seemed to highly dependent on their verbal exchanges, so they talked and talked while Michael continued to elaborate on his own melodramatic past, calling forth memories which he would rather forget. Silently, he hoped his uncensored dialogue would pull at her heartstrings, and they did. But not enough, it seemed, for Kate to do the same with her own bad memories.

For a while, he began talking about his mother's long illness, during which he strongly suspected his mother too had wished for a permanent end to the pain. She'd suffered for the best part of a decade while the cancer had slowly eaten away at her. Prayer didn't help and, in the end, medical intervention had proven to be ineffective. Towards the end, the painkillers had also become nothing but a distraction. Highly sedative and soothing in nature at the beginning, but throughout the years, slowly becoming ineffectual as their effects slowly diminished, leaving them both with nothing but the pain and the anguish which continued to plague them on a daily basis. Those years had become an unending struggle for them, physically and emotionally, but with medical science still stuck somewhere in the Dark Ages, the doctors, despite their many years of study, practice and clinical experience, could do little more than observe as their kind of therapy was laughed at by the aggressive tumours which had spread throughout her body like wildfire.

This was an extremely emotive topic of conversation, but crying out loud, he was consoled by the fact it had diverted his attention away from his withdrawal because he was shaking quite badly now. With every surreptitious glance at the pub doorway, however, his resolve was becoming stronger because, with sobriety, he'd discovered, comes clarity.

Kate's company also hardened his resolve too; her soothing words hitting him violently. However, this form of mental violence was strongly therapeutic, easily showing how the bullshit which had surrounded him and others within his earlier group therapy sessions was cancelled out by her lack of pretension. She seemed utterly committed to pointing out his bullshit excuses through a no holds barred, direct method of scrutiny. Michael was glad of this because he'd relied on lying to himself and ignoring others for far too long now. It would be easy to fall back into this habit, but as he once more glanced at the outside of the pub, it again reminded him of why he wished to remain sober.

Still curious about her familial relationships, Michael ended one of his current disclosures by almost contradicting his earlier thoughts of not pressing her. With his mouth half-open, he bit his tongue. Give her time, he thought as he continued to divulge. The self-absorbed state he found himself submerged in caused him to feel emotionally vulnerable, but he'd felt like this before. The only difference being the fact his heavy disclosures were entirely voluntary. He could have walked away from her, just as he'd walked away from his earlier therapy sessions, deciding, on some level, they were of no use to him and also strongly suspecting the methodology being used could be based on nothing more than a kind of pseudoscience for the gullible. This viewpoint seemed to have served as a justification for his desertion of the therapeutic process. However, after talking to Kate for a little less than a week, Michael had to admit there was some sort of benefit to talking, airing and sharing, so lost in revelation, he talked to the point of distraction while Kate simply nodded her head and encouraged him to continue… and he did.

Talking made him feel better, taking away the shock of withdrawal and giving him a sense of hope and purpose and it soon made him wish for more. However, after finishing off the story of his mother's demise, he realised he was left with nothing more to talk about; he was completely spent. As he realised this, he was surprised to see the sunlight waning. It seemed he had been talking, while she had listened, for half of the afternoon. He felt better now though, so while the sun disappeared over the horizon, he sighed, got to his feet and let go of a few emotions. These were old emotions, remnants left behind from the sadder times, and despite his earlier feelings of caution, he outstretched his arms and embraced her tightly. Things seemed to have moved on for the moment: his withdrawal, his moodiness and, to a certain degree, his cynicism. Kate flinched slightly, so maybe this hug had come as a surprise to her… but it just felt right to him.

Leaving both Kate and the bench behind, he headed back home and continued to cry, letting go for a change and, right at that moment, this change seemed to be for the better.

28

Things soon changed. Having made the decision to take on his mother's need for nursing himself, Michael had rejected any form of outside help from the local doctors. This just seemed right to him. After all, his mother had spent years doing just the same for him and, therefore, he was glad to seize upon the opportunity to pay her back somewhat. This required him to give up his work and he felt a duality of emotion in regards to this: happy, on some level, to be nearer to her, but also sad to let go of the thinking time and independence it had provided.

It wasn't as simple and straightforward as he had thought it would be though. The work was demanding and involved a lot of awkward moments: dressing, undressing, washing, along with dealing out her medications in the right proportions. Too little and she would end up in extreme pain, too much and she would zone out and become incapable of conducting a meaningful conversation with him. Conversations which he always very eagerly looked forward to, finding they were a useful tonic to the feelings of hate and resentment he harboured towards his dad.

The letters continued to arrive, but this time, Michael ignored all of his ravings by leaving them unopened. Instead of burning them, he kept them at arm's length, stacking them neatly within a cupboard located in a corner of his room. There were quite a few of them now, a good couple of dozen, in fact, but decidedly uninterested, he had left them there to gather dust.

He had no inkling of his estranged wife's condition as Michael was named on all of her medical forms as next of kin, avoiding all of the awkwardness which would ensue if he were ever to be informed. Not only did he refuse to give him headspace, he actively continued to leave his father completely out of the loop. This felt good, not only because it was the right thing to do, but also because it pleased him. He would often feel his mood lift whenever he gave it headspace as it further cemented the close relationship which he continued to enjoy with his mother; a relationship which now had very little in the way of barriers. As he became used to the physical aspects of her care, he began to thoroughly enjoy the close bond they both continued to share.

After the initial shock of her collapse, her pain management, the physical side of her care and, whenever she rested, the diligent housework which he immersed himself in effectively diverted his attention away from the fact his mum was slowly dying and, quite actively, he shied away from acknowledging this fact, preferring to occupy himself with nothing more than the essential care which he was very willing to provide. Freud had a word for all of this: denial.

Michael had learnt that ignorance was bliss, so he kept his mind free of all negative thought as he busied himself in his work; never for once giving up the hope of some sort of cure or alleviation for his long-suffering mother. Deep down though, he knew implicitly that this rose-coloured garden of a viewpoint could only be temporary. He was also aware of the pain he himself would feel towards the end. He felt like he was well prepared for this though, which was another lie he frequently told himself. His mother did nothing but praise him, however, doting on her one and only child as he busied himself about her, actively fighting against the truth of the situation.

A meaningful social life, meagre as it had been, soon became impossible for him. His little trips out to the local pub quickly ended, but he didn't miss them, benefitting from the fact the money sitting in his wallet would remain there. They both had a meaningful amount of savings and this, when added to the value of the house, would, even after her death, leave him extremely comfortable. However, he had kept quite a few secrets from her.

On the decidedly rare occasions when he was burnt out, a private carer, which his mum had built up a strong rapport with, would make an overnight stay at their house and allow him the luxury of a night out where he would eagerly make use of all the nearest town had to offer. Drink and the frequent sexual encounters which, he had to admit, were often acquired through cold hard cash gave him a release which was not only pleasurable to him, but was also essential to his mental well-being. Would his mother approve if she had known? He doubted it. But he really couldn't help it. So, with a little guilt, he did what he did and did his best not to dwell on it.

This kind of behaviour would end up forging a certain kind of lifestyle for him. He was completely hedonistic on his nights off, but his little trips out would eventually become a lifestyle habit. This, he would later realise, was all just a setup for his future life without her, but instead of focusing on the future and all of the negativity it contained, they both focused on the present, although the unpleasant aspects of both of their pasts would often intrude. These thoughts would be fleeting though, so for the majority of the time, they lived on in blissful ignorance.

29

Left with nothing else to focus on other than thoughts of his mother's demise, Michael found his long talk with Kate that afternoon now played on his mind. On some level, he felt all the better for it though, so done with crying for now, he sipped coffee in his room, smoked, but also shaked and sweated.

Stuck within the confines of his room, he actively avoided the communal areas of the place. Even though there were no other guests, he was averse to spending any time in his landlady's presence because, within moments, she would undoubtedly notice his physical condition and probably ask questions of him. Questions which he preferred not to answer. Unbeknownst to him, a long night filled with bad dreams awaited him and he was soon held a mental captive of these. His dreams related to not only the sad demise of his mother, but also the harsh and violent treatment he had suffered at the hands of his father, further cementing the fact that, even though he'd left the family home a good few months ago after selling up and heading out on his crazed road trip, his memories would continue to get to him regardless.

Back in his past, while he sat on that old and faithful bench located within the backyard of the house, he let the babble of the stream dampen his thoughts as he shook in both fear and anger. Realising the fact he was impotent, he fought for control, acutely aware of his own weaknesses, but still completely stuck in rumination of this fact. He imagined himself, knife in hand, inflicting slow but mortal damage upon his father, enjoying this as he watched him suffer. Suffer the same kind of pain, anguish and feelings of impotence he frequently bestowed upon both Michael and his mother. This was just a diversion though and he knew it well. Knowing hardly ever changed the concrete facts, however, so tethered to these dualistic non-realities, he, as in his waking life, began to cry.

No one was watching though, so he felt a certain amount of agency, allowing himself this simple expression of emotion and, therefore, caring little of the outside world while he immersed himself in his own self-absorption. With time, these emotions would undoubtedly manifest as behaviour which would, in the main, become very self-destructive, but he knew very little of this yet. So, still stuck as a child in the past, he, quite unwillingly, reminded himself of the day's occurrences.

There had been an argument, over something petty, no doubt, because that's how it always got started. They all knew the truth though; it was just another excuse for him to become violent. After his father had struck his mother a good few times, Michael had somehow drummed up the courage to challenge his dad. It hadn't gone well. His actions had simply infuriated his father further and he was now left with bumps and bruises which would probably take weeks to heal and fade. Although he was feeling it physically, he still felt proud of his little attempt at rebellion, feeling fully justified in his actions and caring little about the consequences. The beating he had taken wasn't the end of the matter though because he knew his dad would continue to punish him for it for days. He knew this implicitly because the fact remained he understood his dad just as well as his mother, both inside and out.

He'd left now, having slammed the front door. He was probably heading to the local boozer to satiate the cravings of what had now become a very resilient physical addiction, so stuck sitting on that old bench, Michael decided to head inside as he was done with crying for now. His mother greeted him in the kitchen, her arms wide open for him, and he hugged her tightly as she consoled him with words. It helped to be near her, to feel the soft comfort of her words and feel her arms tightly gripping him in a loving embrace. There was no substitute for this and Michael kept going back to her, actively seeking her affections, usually after one of his father's episodes.

When he eventually pulled away from her, a few minutes had passed, but instead of his mother's warm, smiling face, another very familiar face smiled back at him. It was Kate's. For a second or two, Michael realised the true meaning behind his dream wasn't completely outside of his grasp. Not a hint, not a teasing clue, but a full-on statement of his hopes and dreams and, as he woke up with the reality of this message, he looked around himself, thinking about nothing more than the potential of his future.

30

That hug, Michael was sure, had been a little premature and, consequently, he felt quite embarrassed about it. So much so that he wished to avoid his newly acquired friend and confidant. Instead of exiting the bed and breakfast, he decided to stay within the safe and cosy confines of his room. After an hour or so, however, he felt restless and a little claustrophobic, so he left to fill up his lungs with fresh air as he scanned the landscape for any potential stressors. Stressors like Kate, that was.

Maybe he was a bit of a coward deep down, but memories of his past behaviour soon clarified this point. Most of his life had consisted of diversions ultimately composed of little more than avoidance tactics. Could this be classed as cowardice or as a completely normal and natural reaction to the dangers which the harsh outside world was filled to the brim with?

He didn't see her though, so as he dropped his cigarette onto the floor, stubbing it out with the heel of his shoe, he found himself once again looking longingly towards the entrance to the local pub, but his resolve hardened. Soon, with his earlier thoughts standing guard, his embarrassment faded and so, having walked purposefully towards that old but symbolic bench, he soon immersed himself in anticipation. Should he full-on apologise for that unasked for embrace or would an apology make things even more awkward and strained between them? He wasn't sure, but he ended up having a long time to think about this.

By early afternoon, he was eventually joined by Kate and her dog Barney. Keeping quiet, as he had decided not to mention that awkward moment of physical contact, he allowed her to talk as, somewhere in the back of his head, he held onto the hope that Kate would open up to him. It took a good couple of hours, but eventually, Michael had successfully steered the conversation away from the potential discussion of his own embarrassment and she started to talk about herself. Firstly, it was her mother who she had taken care of, exactly as he had with his own mother, for so long, but eventually, she disclosed a little about her father, allowing him to share in her pain, disappointment and anger, which just happened to be the exact same emotions Michael had held a tight grip on throughout the decades.

Suddenly, Michael understood the ultimate source of her extreme empathy towards him; her life experience exactly mirrored his own. For a time at least, a deep sense of déjà vu connected the pair. Taken aback, dumbstruck and, for a change, left with nothing else to say, Michael soon discovered her own dad had also been violent, although not to the extent of his own dad. The same feelings existed between them and, still, it continued. The only difference being the fact Kate seemed to have more control over her emotions while she sat there talking, dry-eyed and unfazed by her own words, as Michael listened, finding it was he who was now the encourager. Between her sentences, he found himself nodding at her in anticipation of her next words, anxious to hear the entirety of her story while still holding back on the deep surprise he felt regarding the parallels which seemed to exist between the pair of them.

Thanks to these parallels, Michael got the feeling the both of them now understood each other a lot better than the day before and he was glad to have pushed his embarrassment to one side, realising that hug, far from being an awkward moment, had probably further cemented their bond. Maybe that slight flinch from her hadn't been born out of dislike, but rather served as a catalyst for acceptance. She hadn't mentioned, or even hinted at, any past romantic relationships, and the fact remained that Michael still knew nothing about her sexuality. This further demonstrated the, hitherto, one-sided nature of their non-physical relationship, but this had now changed.

In an effort to console her, he offered her his hand as she now, once again, focused on her mother, talking in an accepting tone about all of her suffering. She didn't seem to apportion blame though. Neither to God nor any other living soul, like he surely did, and seemed to have successfully dealt with these emotional barriers. Talking quite openly, she continued, but Michael couldn't help but feel slightly weaker than her. Had his hate and resentment made him an inferior person? Had the exact religion, which he had seen nothing but hypocrisy in, been the clincher for her? This certainly seemed to be the case and, while her grip tightened on his hand, he ended up feeling a little ashamed of the dismissive and completely hedonistic behaviour which lay in his past. It embarrassed him, in fact. Left a little deflated, he held her hand somewhat tighter as she continued on with her disclosure while feelings of empathy and mental affection washed over him.

She wasn't done talking yet though and she soon elaborated further on her past as she admitted she had been mostly a loner as a child; a state of being which had continued well into her adult life. Michael was shocked. Surely someone as switched on as her should have several friendships under her belt? Elaborating further, she also disclosed the fact that, for most of her life, she had been an observer, falling into that constant habit of simply connecting the behaviour of others with their words and actions. Again, Michael could strongly empathise with this, but soon came to the conclusion that his own belief system had been based on nothing more than hate, fear and cynicism wherein he had often wrongly identified the motives, and motivations, of others and, for a while, he wondered whether Kate's pragmatism could be catching.

She still sported that old, and highly symbolic, badge which had been pinned to her coat: that outline of a fish denoting the fact she was a practising Christian. But even though his outlook now had a chance of changing, he suspected his lack of faith was probably incorrigible in nature. His mother had drummed a lot of religion into him, making him learn scripture, sing hymns and worship this ultimate father figure in the sky, but to Michael, this particular being had a lot in common with his own father; the only difference being that, instead of violent abuse, this enduring and highly symbolic father figure routinely dealt out an even harsher form of abuse: apathy. So, as he sat there, holding Kate's hand, he realised there were limits to his own spiritual awakening because, despite having forgiven his father, he continued to feel abandoned by God.

Kate's interjection into his life now felt more like an adoption, but he knew implicitly that had his mother been alive right at this moment, she would undoubtedly propose that God himself had sent Kate as a messenger to help him change his ways before he killed himself through his limitless consumption of alcohol. Deep down, Michael knew he would immediately reject this notion. He had next to no belief invested in fate either, so he, rather stubbornly, took her intervention to be down to simple good luck or to complete chance.

Sitting there, these thoughts shot through his mind while he continued to listen and absorb. Kate now seemed exhausted though, her words slowly trailing off as he painfully wished for more, but soon realising she had given all she could for that one day. Once more, the sun waned, disappearing over the horizon while a nearby streetlight took over the job; a weaker and slightly less effective light source. With a lot said, digested and understood, they parted company; the both of them silently hoping for more during the course of the following day.

Back in his room, Michael soon found the shakes were a little more tolerable now, but the familiarity of his cravings persisted. It had been a good four days of sobriety, but these shakes, along with his unwavering craving for the demon booze, hung on tightly, causing a certain amount of anxiety. Anxiety over whether he could successfully push his body over the finishing line. He now guessed he was probably halfway through this figurative marathon, but through observation and experience, he knew he'd probably be running alongside temptation for many years to come.

The walls within his room were slowly closing in now and not just metaphorically either. He could see them waxing and waning as if they were losing substance and knew, quite certainly, he had begun to hallucinate again. Hoping to avoid what his eyes told him was completely real, he concentrated on his thoughts which quickly told him what wasn't. Regarding the former, the only option he had was to sleep, so climbing into bed, he neglected to strip down to his underwear and lay there fully clothed and attempted to drift off. It wasn't happening though, so after a while, he realised that, combined with the undulating sight of the walls which seemed to ebb and flow, an entirely understandable physical reaction became that of nausea.

Now, happy with the fact he had remained fully clothed, he found himself exiting his room and rushing towards the upstairs toilet. Once there, he dropped to his knees and vomited, retching and bringing up, it seemed, a lot more than he had actually consumed.

Kneeling there, he tried to calm himself, telling himself loudly that his withdrawal was only temporary, but this took nothing away from the reality of the situation. His body was fighting him, eager for the intoxicating chemicals it had gotten so used to despite the fact those same chemicals had poisoned every part of his body by killing brain cells and fattening and enlarging his liver. Alcohol: a handy pick-me-up which, if he were to continue to use and abuse it, would eventually kill him, doubtlessly in an excruciating and highly painful way. He couldn't stay where he was though, so swaying like the walls were, he successfully made it back to his room, locked the door and sauntered over to his bed. Sleep came quickly this time and he painfully welcomed it, shutting his eyes and drifting off, smothering the nerve cells in his brain which were aggravated by the fact their cravings had not been satiated. Unused to this sober state, they continued to rebel, calling loudly to him for another fix while he ignored these loaded requests and drifted off.

It had been a very productive day, but despite all of this, it had ended on a downer. As he was embraced by sleep, he allowed the more pleasant aspects of the day to overtake his thoughts.

31

❖

The following morning, not knowing whether he had dreamt or not, Michael awoke to find the previous night's shakes had returned, but he just ignored them. Instead of going through his normal, run of the mill morning routine, he just sat there in the chair facing the window and was soon lost in thought.

Had Kate now taken over the role his mother had adopted, quite exclusively, decades earlier? Right now, he seemed to both need and crave this kind of attention, but couldn't quite seem to metaphorically sever the maternal heartstrings which had, throughout his youth, grounded him in reality. As these memories, which were highly pleasurable in nature, passed through his mind, he began thinking about nothing more than the better times. These consisted, in the main, of the years following his father's sweet departure from the household; times when Michael had largely served as a full-time confidant and carer for his ailing mother. Suddenly, the outside world didn't seem so harsh because, right then, his mind began to focus almost entirely on these much happier times.

Suddenly, his shakes and general malaise were pushed to the back of his mind as he lost himself in memories; memories which seemed to cancel out any present negativity. Totally immersed inside his own thoughts, he found himself focusing on Kate and the hope that she would soon become a conduit which would help him process all the harsh, and highly melodramatic, aspects of his past. As he focused on this, so much so that his normal morning dose of nicotine and caffeine were easily forgotten, he began to daydream quite deeply; so deeply he didn't even hear the knock on his door until it was rather loudly repeated.

Getting back to reality, Michael strode over to the door, soon finding his physical condition, reflected back to him in the mirror attached to the rear wall, showed him as a shell of his former self. Quite suddenly, he noticed his shakes, cravings and general demeanour had taken a nose-dive, so rather reluctantly, he pulled open his door and was confronted with the welcoming sight of Kate.

Her look of surprise soon transferred to that of concern though as she proceeded to cross over the threshold and into his room. For a second or two, while he closed the door, she just stared back at him.

She eventually said, "We need to get you some help." She was soon suggesting a trip to see the local doctor.

For a second, but only for a split second or so, he was about to disagree, to just brush the suggestion off offhandedly, but after taking another look at himself in the mirror, he quickly realised that, not only was seeing a healthcare professional a good idea, but that it could also be an extremely sensible one too.

Therefore, instead of flopping down on a chair or crashing out on the room's only bed, he reached for his coat and, rather embarrassingly, ended up walking past his landlady in the outside corridor while she busied herself about the place. She said nothing, just stared with surprise at his current condition. Thankfully, they ventured outside and were soon heading inexorably towards a red Fiat Punto parked just a couple of streets away from the entrance to the place.

Luckily, Kate possessed both a car and a valid driving licence, so with the local GP practice being a town away, she drove a pinch too fast as he continued on with his shakes and sweats which were also, as before, accompanied by an intolerable craving for alcohol. Thanks to the pace at which she drove, they both reached the practice within a relatively short space of time.

Parking up in a small carpark, she brought the Punto to a stop. Still shaking, quite uncontrollably now,

Michael shuffled over towards the entrance, passing through the main door as that morning's secretary stared ahead of herself, focusing on nothing more than the "admissions" list which was doubtlessly relayed to her desktop computer. Upon seeing them both, her eyes slightly widened and she was soon booking him in to see the resident doctor in "about half an hour" she was soon stating, following their request for a rough estimate of the waiting time.

There were a few others scattered around the waiting room, which ultimately made it even worse for him, and he sat there, beside Kate, wishing he was invisible. Part of this was related to the fact he felt a little guilty as he sat there, taking up the time of both the doctor and his underlings given the fact his condition was completely self-inflicted. However, nothing but worry was evident on Kate's face. It expressed concern; concern that he might just keel over right next to her, he guessed. Michael's will negated this possibility because the fact remained that he was just too stubborn to start giving up, so rather painfully, he continued to sit and wait his turn as chart music blared out of a small handheld radio which resided somewhere within the reception area of the place.

True to the receptionist's estimate, he was seen by the resident doctor within half an hour of his arrival and Michael eventually found himself sitting down on one of two chairs facing his desk. With one short look at him, the doctor was soon scribbling out a prescription which could be redeemed at the local chemist, but still insisted on questioning him on the plainly visible results of decades worth of drinking, asking what his "average" intake of alcohol had been and even the reasons behind his addiction. Totally unnecessary as this was, Michael was unfazed and he answered all of the doctor's short and rapid questions in an almost automatic, hypnotic and uncensored way while he stared back at him with, surprisingly, an unmistakable look of sympathy present on his face. Michael's extreme embarrassment slowly began to fade.

Getting to the local chemist pretty swiftly, Michael soon handed over a prescription for Valium, an infamous, small, blue-coloured pill with an individual strength of ten milligrams. With the rather unnecessary rigmarole over with, he was soon downing two of these blue-coloured pills in the parking lot with a bottle of orange juice which Kate had tucked away inside the glovebox of her car, already ingesting half of the recommended daily dose prescribed to him by the doctor.

The pills would take a while to kick in, even on an empty stomach, but Michael didn't mind this and, as they neared home, having booked a follow-up appointment for the following week, they passed through a small patch of the harsh landscape he just so happened to have walked a substantial length of a few days before. In silence though. Nothing needed to be said now Michael had, once more, accepted the help offered to him by a relative stranger. Talking was one thing, but admitting to an addiction in the hope of a tonic could be hard work. He'd ignored what remained of his pride that morning though and seemed to have reaped the benefit of this. He soon realised Kate's concern for him now seemed even stronger than he had previously guessed it to be, which provided him with a depth of comfort he hadn't felt in years. He mentally thanked her for this, but admittedly, non-verbally. He did this because he wasn't too sure what her reaction would be. Losing all of these thoughts though, he realised he would have to face his new landlady when they returned and was decidedly nervous about what *her* reaction would be.

Having reached the small hamlet, Michael, a little less concerned now following the silence of the short ride home, re-entered the building. Luckily, they didn't encounter her either in the lobby, staircase, or in the meandering corridor, so having reached his room, he proceeded to sit down on the very edge of the bed while Kate took up position on the chair facing the window.

Now he was safely ensconced inside his own room, Michael felt extremely thankful for her help, but the fact remained that he had been just too habitually pig-headed to seek the help of others for so long now and he mentally reprimanded himself for this. Sitting on the edge of the bed, he accepted his arrogant and stubborn nature as Kate flipped the switch on the kettle and made them both a strong coffee, but as she did so, Michael started to feel the effect of the pills upon him. He felt calm, serene even, but he also found that, despite this sudden feeling, he was still craving for something a tad stronger than the coffee she served. However, a streak of selfishness simultaneously made him wish for Kate's absence. Despite what she had done for him throughout that morning, he longed for his own company. He said nothing of this though, just sat there while she served up a mug of coffee and sat down on the room's only chair, dragging it away from the window to solidly face him.

All he said was "thank you", but it seemed she was angry at him. Maybe that was why he had wanted her gone. Seeing her stern-looking face, he again sensed her burgeoning fury. Instead of communicating her feelings directly to him though, she just sat there, staring back at him in an unflinching and unwavering way.

Maybe he should break the silence, but he felt disinclined to do so. He just sat there sipping at his coffee, avoiding her gaze as several thoughts flipped through his mind. One of which was the possibility that she had thought he should have asked for her help long before that day, but she had seen the state of him for quite a while now, so why hadn't she suggested him seeing a doctor long before that day? Would he have dismissed her though? *Probably* was the answer he gave to himself, provided by that small, critical voice inside his head which, for time immemorial, had followed him around, seemingly focused on nothing more than admonishing him whenever the opportunity arose.

Hoping to deflect this unhappy voice, and to lighten the mood a little, he said, "I was stupid."

Holding her gaze on him, she blurted out an affirmative. 'Extremely!"

Michael offered nothing more though, just a nod as he sipped away at his coffee.

Kate did the same while Michael began thinking about whether there was any way, short of the apology he had just made, he could diffuse the situation. But there wasn't, so he just stayed silent. Eventually, and after he had expressed another weak apology and a strong thank you, Kate finished off her coffee and strode out of the room without any further comment on the negative feelings she now obviously harboured towards him.

She'd cool off though, he thought as he was left alone.

Suddenly, he felt tired, but he didn't think this was the effect of the pills. Rather, his emotional vulnerability had left him weak, helpless and a little depressed, so highly aware of this fact, he crashed out on his bed and attempted to dull his senses. Something which had been quite easy in the past through his heavy drinking, so while the cravings returned, he reminded himself all about the oath he had made to himself. This was just a dry patch, he thought and, during this thought, he drifted off.

32

He wasn't dreaming much recently, he discovered, while he woke up later that night. He'd slept, but the old dreams which had haunted him for so long had hardly manifested for a good few days now. He concluded that, in the past, these dreams had probably been instigated by his heavy and habitual drinking, but as he downed another couple of blue pills, he sat on the chair by the window and looked out across the town which was now blanketed in fog. The sickly orange glare of the streetlights easily cut through this, but as he lit up a cigarette, he didn't seem to be burdened by all the negativity that had become a lifelong companion of his. All in all, he felt, to some degree anyway, proud to have faced his extreme fear of rejection head on, realising he had drowned this fear in alcohol since forever. At times, he had thought people were just as uncaring as he had been and, therefore, had excused his own selfish actions through thinking in this way. He soon surrounded himself with a few home truths, anxiously grasping on to this fact and coming to the unwavering conclusion that his anxiety had also been frequently quashed by a heavy and sustained dose of alcohol.

While he just sat there, he also sensed, following other similar thoughts, that his newly acquired feelings towards others had been generated by their increasingly kind actions towards him. Kate being a prime example. Quite suddenly, he found himself latching on to the wish to appease her in some way, now he had sussed out the source of her anger. For a while, he simply sat there, contemplating this while the Valium took effect. He was soon leaving his seat, undressing and flopping down on his bed, simultaneously realising the sweats and shakes had, for a time at least, stopped. After an hour or so, and still in a philosophical state of mind, he came to realise how tired he had become, so surrendering himself once more to sleep, he closed his eyes as the room became dark.

33

❖

That need to appease stayed with him as he awoke with a far clearer head than he'd had the previous day. Starting it off with a few smokes and a strong black coffee, he also realised that, once more, he hadn't dreamt. However, although they had seemed to have disappeared for a while the night before, his shakes had returned. They weren't as harsh as they had been, but Michael was soon reaching for his little bottle of blue pills and downing a couple of them with a few sips of coffee. Hopefully, by the time he headed out, they would have subsided to a more manageable level.

There was still that question regarding his landlady though and he felt a little anxious about this, but knew implicitly that that upcoming encounter would be impossible to avoid. He simply didn't know what excuse he could give her to placate her obvious curiosity because, during the course of that short encounter with her the day before, all he had seen was just that. Along with a little snoopiness. Having other guests which she could have been distracted by would have been a slightly safer option, but with him being the sole occupier of the business, her attention seemed to be unwaveringly focused upon him. With these concerns in mind, Michael continued to drink and smoke, delaying going out. At least until the little blue pills had taken some sort of effect on him.

An hour had soon passed and, at present, the pills seemed to be doing their job, so with the deep need to appease Kate uppermost on his mind, he strode out of the door, hardly flinching as he passed by his landlady. In fact, even slipping by her with a cheery "good morning" emanating from his lips. He certainly looked better than he had the day before and, after a while, he felt brighter… brighter than he in fact looked, but still more "with it" than he had ever been. He thought of just scouting for Kate's car instead of waiting for her at the bench because he was now anxious to see where she lived, but was unsure of this. Although the ageing bench had served as an adequate backdrop to their budding relationship before now, Michael wasn't too sure about whether trying to appease her on her home ground would be a good idea. He certainly didn't want to feel like he was intruding, so changing direction, he backtracked the short distance which he had covered to sit silently upon that withering old bench. Were they approaching an argument or a small tiff, ultimately brought on by his stubbornness? Or would Kate's anger towards him have subsided by now?

Voices, loud and brash, soon came from the rear as the punters at the local bar popped out for their cigarettes and Michael stared behind him and in their general direction, realising his longing for a drink had faded along with his shakes. Just seeing them happy, jolly and highly intoxicated would, hitherto, have made him crave a drink, but although still craving, he realised this craving was just about tolerable now. Continuing to stare, he began to feel about as paranoid as he had been just a few days ago. Were the jokes on him? He quickly admonished himself for thinking in this way and, with these thoughts still active in his mind, he was surprised to find both Kate and her pooch standing smack bang in front of him as he slowly turned himself around.

Her hands were on her hips, which wasn't a good sign, but she soon spoke to him.

"You're only looking like death half warmed-up today," she stated.

Eager to voice his apologies, he said, "About yesterday…" but he failed to elaborate.

She simply shook her head though. "I've reminded myself that you *are* redeemable."

Not disguising his relief, Michael exhaled all of the air he had been holding in and simply said, "Good," while wanting to hold her once more.

However, she just stood there, weighing him up, he supposed, but fairly soon, she sat beside him and smiled.

"How's Kelly?" she asked.

"Who's Kelly?"

Kate held her smile, elaborating. "Your landlady… Ms Harding?"

Michael, having been a little perplexed, understood now she had clarified and said, "I didn't stop to talk, but she seems a wee bit curious."

"Nosy, you mean?" Kate countered.

Michael couldn't help but smile. "Yeah, extremely nosy."

"But that's exactly how people are around here!" she elaborated, then added, "Including me, I suppose?"

It took a while for Michael to understand that her comment had been some sort of a challenge, but despite the delay, he was soon answering her.

"You're not nosy, just concerned," he said, before adding, "I assume so anyway."

Kate, looking a little hurt, replied with, "You're right to assume."

They sat in silence for a while, saying and doing nothing much of anything but staring out across the loch until Kate spoke again.

"You're not shaking as much today."

"The miracles of modern medicine," Michael answered, once more grateful for her interest and concern.

"You still miss it though?"

Michael assumed the drink was what she was referring to and said, "Over the last day or so, I'd have to say that not as much as before."

"Good," was all she said, confirming the fact she had meant the drink. "Fancy a walk?"

"I really fancy breakfast, in all honesty," he said, and they were soon walking through the entrance to the local cafe.

The cafe was welcoming towards Barney, barring any of the other customers complaining over his presence, but since there were only the three of them there, the proprietor Sally had no such complaints. She even provided a bowlful of water which she placed onto the ground next to the pooch. Having ordered up some dry toast for her and a hearty full English breakfast for him, they both watched on while the dog lapped at the water; obviously very thirsty.

After a second or two, Kate knelt over and started stroking him rather affectionately and in the same way Michael had during their recent exchange: running her long, manicured fingers through his thick coat and talking softly to him.

Michael smiled as he took in the scene. He hadn't had the time to begin to feel any sort of affection towards the mutt, but he could see why a fair few owners became so attached to their pets. Being emotionally sterile for as long as he had, maybe his new openness towards other people was fuelling these thoughts, he thought as she continued to fuss over her much-loved pet.

Their food swiftly arrived and Michael was soon tucking in, making short work of his breakfast due to the fact he was now extremely hungry, while Kate took her time with her dry toast. Looking down, he noticed the dog wasn't begging and he quickly commented on this.

"You've got him well-trained."

Looking up, she said, "All thanks go to Pavlov for that one."

That little bit of psychology got him thinking about how he himself had been conditioned; conditioned to not expect too much from his fellow man. That thought soon cut through his cheerful mood, making him feel a little depressed over all the years he had wasted in ignorance and in the insatiable pursuit of pleasure. Barring a couple of episodes, such as that long-winded chat about his past he'd had with Claire, that Glasgow prostitute, just a few months ago, he had allowed his past to strongly influence his thoughts, actions and behaviour, thinking nothing about wasting his potential.

Had things settled down for him now? Were there any other options open to him? Or was his break from the drinking only temporary? The answers to all of these questions alluded him, but he decided to just wait and see. Instead of stressing about his future, he finished off his meal while he glanced up at Kate, as she slowly sipped away at her coffee, trying to weigh her up. Was it time to start settling down? Maybe without Kate? Was their relationship just temporary? Just a fleeting encounter which would aid him in reaching another point in his, until now, miserable life which had been marred by extreme addiction? If so, were there greener pastures awaiting him?

These were questions which, during the past week or so, had flitted through his mind whilst he had fought those extreme cravings and attempted to accept the side effects of a drug withdrawal and shift in lifestyle alongside the mental effects of a change in perspective and, as he sat there, still trying to break the silence with some sort of meaningful comment, Michael decided to allow life to give him another shot; he was owed that much at least.

Printed in Great Britain
by Amazon

59295177R00091